Last Stop Before Heaven

A Novel By

Sylvia Martin Vega

DISCLAIMER

This is a work of fiction and all characters are products of the author's imagination, as is the fictional facility called the Florida Forest. Any resemblance to persons living or dead, or any facilities presently or previously operating, is purely coincidental.

"Honor the aged for they are, above all else, survivors."
Scribbled on the bathroom stall in the Nurse's Lounge
at the Florida Forest, circa 1994.

DEDICATION

To old women everywhere.

PART ONE

It was dawn and all Mary wanted to do was to take her hair down and put her feet up.

Mary was working a "double". She had reported for a shift at 2:30 yesterday afternoon and had worked through the crashing sounds of the dinner tray pass, the subterranean sounds of steamy showers, the endless drone of television sets at deafening decibels and finally, silence.

It was then, in this still silent period, that the staff rested, sipping thick black coffee out of thin white cups and listening, no longer consciously, for the first sound to break the stillness.

But it was dawn now, and Mary was to help dress three residents (don't ever call them patients), early risers who went to the main dining hall for first breakfast. And now, only Dolly was left and then Mary could do change-of-shift rounds and go home.

"Tired, honey?" Dolly asked her when she entered the room.

It's getting pretty bad, Mary thought, if the residents were asking that question of her. Well, in a few more months, she could stop working these damned double shifts.

"A little," she answered.

"Don't be a fool, honey," Dolly told her. "Don't kill yourself working."

Tired as she was, Mary grinned as she picked up the hairbrush to style Dolly's long, magnificent locks. "And if I ever stopped breaking my butt around here, Dolly, you would be the first to complain."

"The first and the loudest," Dolly agreed. "But so what? So an old woman complains, you gonna kill yourself working so an old woman won't complain?"

Mary didn't answer. Instead, she brushed out Dolly's waist length, white gold hair. Her hair reminded Mary of the silky blonde hair of the prom queens and cheerleaders that she had gone to high school with. It was hard to believe that such hair belonged to an 85-year-old woman.

After Mary had expertly twisted Dolly's hair into a "honeybun" she brought the mirror for Dolly's inspection. Dolly stared at her face for a brief moment and nodded.

"Well, that's about as good as it's going to get, I suppose."

"Dolly, you're beautiful," Mary said. She meant it. Dolly had smooth, amazingly unlined skin, the color of warm cinnamon and bright eyes, the color of coals. And she was so tiny. Mary never could get over how small her hands and feet were.

"Well, my mother was black and my father was white," Dolly began, and Mary fought the urge to mouth the words behind Dolly's head before Dolly could speak them. It was Dolly's story, and she told it endlessly, repeatedly, so many times a day that most people assumed that she was a little crazy. Mary didn't care if Dolly was crazy or not, but she didn't think that she was. Listening, she emptied Dolly's wash basin and gathered the soiled laundry for the day's laundry.

"And a half-white woman had no more rights than a black woman, but that didn't hardly matter, seeing how a white woman had no more rights than a black woman, anyhow," Dolly was saying. Mary listened for the part that came next, the part about how, for that matter, a black man had no more rights than any woman did, but instead, Dolly stopped suddenly and laughed outright.

3

"What's funny, Dolly?"

"All these years. All these years, I waited on white folks and now, white folks are waiting on me."

"You're not so crazy, are you Dolly?"

"No honey. Not nearly as crazy as they think I am."

****

NURSING RULE #1: If it wasn't charted, it wasn't done.

****

Stella Vaughn rose with the sun. It wasn't as if she had to, or even wanted to anymore. It was just something that she did.

The evening aide had left her curtains partway open, the way she liked them. This way, when she woke up, she could watch the first sun of the day splash over the palms and hibiscus and banana trees that grew up and over the veranda that her window led to. Stella loved the way that the lush greenery made everything look like a deep primeval forest, even on the brightest summer day. She longed to leap out of her bed and fling the window open, inhaling the moist, flowery morning

4

air, but it wasn't so easy anymore. Stella was 103 years old.

Content instead she had to be with looking at the morning from her bed, waiting patiently for the day aide to help her. For the evening girl, who had so thoughtfully left her curtains open, had also left Stella's walker about two feet out of her reach.

Stella didn't mind. These girls were young, with limber, strong bodies that didn't ache every time they moved. They tried hard, most of them, but they couldn't understand what it was to be old. Sometimes, they made mistakes simply because they didn't think like old people.

To pass the time, Stella examined her legs. They were very thin now, and very white, with hundreds of twisting tortuous purple varicosities. They reminded Stella of a road map and she could look at them, fascinated, never truly believing that they were her legs.

Remembering now, she fell back against the pillows, closing her eyes to conjure back a time when her legs had been long and strong and tanned and gorgeous. "Legs", they had once called her, or "Stems". She remembered pumps and stilettos and silk stockings and lace garters. She remembered how much else a man could forgive in a woman if she had beautiful legs.

****

NURSING RULE #10: Chart in black ink only, never blue.

****

Ellen had always wanted to be a nurse.

Growing up as she did, the classic dysfunctional family triangle of love, booze and violence, Ellen had felt completely powerless for most of her childhood. Then, one morning, at the age of twelve, Ellen stepped into the small bathroom that the family shared and grabbed her toothbrush. Ignoring her brother's pounding on the closed door, she glanced up into the mirror above the chipped porcelain sink.

What she saw caused her to nearly bite her toothbrush in half and prompted her to cry out, "Mama, come quick! You won't believe this."

And Ellen's mother, after pushing Ellen's brother aside, rushed into the bathroom. She took one look at her only daughter and burst into tears.

Ellen had gone to sleep skinny and plain and awkward and had woken up unforgivably beautiful.

6

Soon followed the breasts and the hips and the boys. And for the first time in her life, Ellen knew she had power.

She might have grown obnoxious if it were not for her clinical interest in how the human body worked. The novelty of being the prettiest girl in the neighborhood grew thin, and she became bored with it. Other girls, not quite as pretty as Ellen, garnered most of the attention. They were friendlier, more vivacious, and they dressed better. Ellen became more or less a loner.

In her junior year of high school, she met Jim Patrick. Soon afterward, she was pregnant. By then, Ellen was convinced that she probably wasn't bright enough to complete an intensive nursing program anyway.

Ellen was often impatient with her daughter, which made her certain she lacked the patience to become a nurse. Mistakes she made with her child convinced her she lacked common sense. Finally, at the age of 30, she ran out of excuses. Going quietly insane in a climate-controlled insurance office, surrounded by hundreds of color paper clips and sticky memo pads, she decided.

"That's it. I am going to do it. I'm going to be a nurse."

Her life, she vowed, was going to make a difference.

****

NURSING RULE #23: There is no such thing as a democracy in a freshman nursing class.

****

As Ellen approached the front door of the nursing school on that first day, she recognized three women she remembered from her prerequisite classes. They acknowledged one another and walked into the building and up the stairs together. By the time they reached the top of the stairs they had already confided their hopes to each other.

Ellen was already acquainted with Stacey, an agency nurse's aide who sometimes worked at the Florida Forest with Ellen. The nursing school's background check revealed that Stacy was also known as "Sugar Babe."

"Sugar Babe?" Ellen asked.

"I was a topless dance for three years."

"Stacey!" gasped Kelly.

"Americans are so hung up on sex. In the Netherlands, it is not such a big deal," offered Beth.

"Oh no," Kelly said. "I couldn't do that."

"I could if I had to," replied Ellen.

****

Nursing school began with a math test that eliminated yet another five students from a class barely born, and from there, it got worse.

The first few months of any nursing program is a weeding out process. Most students were weeded out for either academic or attendance failure, but a few were weeded out because they did not grasp that there is no such thing as democracy in a freshman nursing class. Kelly came close to being thrown out for the first reason, and Stacey came even closer for the last reason.

"Why don't you learn to be quiet?" Beth asked. "You can't win with her."

"She's not going to talk to me like that," Stacey answered.

"She wouldn't if you'd shut up," interjected Ellen. "Look, like it or not, she's the instructor, and she decides who lives and who dies in this program."

"You guys, quit arguing and help me," cried a frustrated Kelly. "I only got an 81 on Skeletal. Passing is 80."

"Well, you'd do better if you didn't go clubbing every weekend," Ellen noted.

"Hey, I need a break," Kelly protested. "I'm still young. I need to party."

Kelly was young. At 20, she was the youngest in a class of 50 students. By the sophomore block, only 27 students had not been asked to leave. Ellen, Kelly, Stacey and Beth were among them. They were still standing.

****

NURSING RULE #32: Never chart that an Incident Report has been filed.

****

The Florida Forest was a sprawling 500-bed, hurricane-safe facility set on a dozen wooded acres. Billed as "Florida's Finest Skilled Nursing & Rehabilitation Center," it sat perilously close to the interstate. Perilous, that is, for those residents given to wandering, but that is not what visitors notice first about the place. They noticed the Olympic-sized swimming pool, the courtyards, the gazebos and the verandas. There was a chapel, a store, a beauty salon and a meeting hall. Meals were good and the facility was clean. All in all, it wasn't a bad place to live, providing you had the mental and physical means to enjoy the amenities.

Stella Vaughn had the means. She used her walker as much as possible, relying on the wheelchair only when she was in a hurry. This morning, she was in a hurry.

"Don't you want your breakfast, Miss Vaughn?"

"No darling, I'm not hungry," Stella said to Tasha, the aide. Tasha was a plump, sweet-faced young girl and her brown wrinkled in concern.

"Are you feeling okay, Miss Vaughn?"

"Never felt better. Hand me my lipstick, will you honey?"

Tasha handed Stella a silver filigreed lipstick case and watched as the ancient woman slowly, tremblingly opened the case and raised a violent shade of fushia to her lips.

"Spray my bosom with Chanel, will you baby?"

****

Clinical started in November, leaving Ellen and Kelly on one side of town and Beth and Stacey on the other. The women now met only once weekly for classes.

Ellen did very well in clinical. Her poise made her the envy of her classmates, and only Ellen knew that she threw up every clinical morning.

Kelly was late for clinical twice and was placed on probation.

Stacey was asked to leave her clinical site for the rest of the day one day in December because, as she said, "She took an attitude with me."

Beth, who was probably top of her class at this point, said only, "Americans make such a show of everything.

****

Stella was in a hurry to catch Robert Bishop before he went into the Resident Council Meeting. Tall with bright blue eyes, he reminded her of John, her fifth and favorite husband.

"Morning, Mrs. Vaughn."

"Good morning, Mr. Bishop. I hear they're playing Casablanca this afternoon. Would you happen to know what time it starts?"

12

"Oh, you're going to see that?"

"Yes indeed. Wouldn't miss it."

"It starts at two o'clock. Would you be so kind as to meet me at half past one for a coffee? I mean, if you don't already have other plans."

"It would be my pleasure, Mr. Bishop."

****

That done, Stella had little else to do. She still wasn't hungry, and Activities didn't start until nine o'clock.

She wheeled herself out of the front lobby, nodding to the pretty young receptionist on the way out. Stella noticed how many other residents used the footrest of their wheelchairs even when they didn't have to. Stella preferred to use her feet to help propel the chair as it saved her the strain on her arms.

Once outside in the morning sun, Stella grew drowsy and dozed, the Chanel diffusing into a world of brightly colored birds and honeybees and flowers that blossomed even when snowflakes fell everywhere else in the country.

****

NURSING RULE #68: Never administer a syringe that you didn't draw up yourself.

****

The first clinical had taken place in a nursing home, one not nearly as spacious and accommodating as the Florida Forest.

The second clinical took place in a hospital. It was soon to be known as The Rotation from Hell. For one thing, it was to be the longest rotation of the program. For another, there were nurses placed there specifically to torment nursing students.

One Tuesday in January, Kelly missed clinical. Ellen felt a mixture of concern and annoyance. For the first time ever, Ellen was late, owing to a flat tire. She arrived during the lecture with a faint grease stain on her blindingly white scrub pants. She took her place next to Beth, who looked deathly pale.

Ellen looked around. She knew that Stacey was doing makeup work in the lab. But where was Kelly? She'd never pass if she kept missing time.

"Have you heard anything from Kelly?" she whispered to Beth.

"I'll talk to you at the break," Beth answered tightly. And at the break, Beth lit a cigarette and spoke softly and quickly, her accent so thick that morning that Ellen could barely understand her. Ellen had never seen Beth smoke.

"I got a phone call last night from a friend that Kelly and I both work with. They found a body in a hotel, and they think it's Kelly."

And Ellen did not comprehend, not at first. She went back to class with a loud hum in her ears. And when the instructor whispered to Beth and Beth's eyes filled with tears, Ellen did not respond. For the next one and one-half hours, Ellen and Beth sat mutely glued to their seats, taking notes nearly verbatim. Years later, when Ellen looked back at her notes for that day, she saw that some of the words spanned three lines. But Ellen and Beth never stopped writing.

And at 11:00, right before the lunch break, the woman knew what the instructor had to tell the class before she spoke.

****

Kelly's death caused her classmates to cry. Whether they had liked her or not or even known her, most of them cried.

15

She had, according to the police report, checked into a motel early that Tuesday morning and asked not to be disturbed. She swallowed an entire bottle of tranquilizers and slipped into a full bathtub. An investigation revealed no evidence of foul play. It appeared as if Kelly had chosen to do this and had not told anyone why.

Stacey probably took it the hardest. She stopped speaking to Ellen and Beth.

Ellen and Beth pulled closer together. They never spoke of Kelly again after that first awful week.

In April, they finally left The Rotation from Hell. Ellen was glad to be rid of anything that reminded her of Kelly.

****

The Florida Forest had stood for 30 years, making it one of the oldest structures in the area. Hundreds, maybe thousands of residents had passed through its' grandiose carved double doors over the past three decades. For most, it was their last stop before Heaven.

Mary was not afraid of the death that was common to her work. Residents died in her arms, the transition eased (she hoped) by her low voice and gentle touch. Afterward, she would close their eyes and their mouths and comb their hair. Mary found nothing weird or creepy in this final stage of patient care.

Mary Drennan had been a nurse's aide for 17 years. She was not afraid of much. She was a common sense, down to Earth type of woman, the kind that many of her residents referred to as "the salt of the Earth." Mary had spiritual beliefs that included Heaven and Hell and an Afterlife. She would have liked to attend church regularly, but her job required that she work most Sunday mornings.

Nonetheless, Mary was not the type of woman to put much belief in the ghost stories that circulated throughout the Florida Forest, legends that exist in any place that has housed so many souls during the transition from life to death. Mary didn't believe the odd tales whispered among the nurses and the aides. Not at first, anyway.

Once, however, she entered a resident's room just in time to see an angel vanish over the bed. Or at least, it looked like what Mary and most of us would assume to be an angel. The resident, a woman in her final days of bone cancer, looked, for once, radiantly rested. The strange thing was that Mary was not startled. Even though she had never seen such a thing, it was as if that were the most natural thing in the world for her to see. The next day, the woman died.

For five of her 17 years of nursing, Mary had worked on the Sunshine Unit, the Florida Forest's locked unit. Few residents died there as locked unit's residents are generally very active.

Mary never forgot Grace, the pleasant woman from Upstate New York. Every locked unit has one resident who doesn't seem to belong, who demonstrates enough cognitive ability to make the staff wonder What In The Hell Is She Doing Here? Grace was such a resident.

Grace used to take long walks along the secured corridors and outdoor courtyards. She looked longingly at the unit's only door that led to the outside world, the one door she could not exit through.

"I don't know why I am locked up here. Not that it's not a place because it is, dear, but I don't know why I am locked up here."

And Mary didn't know either. At that time, Mary had eight residents that she cared for. With seven of them, Mary knew why they were there. But with Grace, she did not.

Quite suddenly, Grace died. The Sunshine Unit buzzed with ghost stories.

"Nonsense," Mary said.

"Mary," Rose put her hand on Mary's arm. "I've been an aide for 20 years, so you figure how many I've seen die, and I have never felt what I feel in her room. Go in there. I'm not kidding, Mary, she's in that room."

"Screw you," Mary replied cheerfully. "You go in there." And all of the other aides laughed, and that was that. But two days later, they ended up working disorganized (We are not working short, the staff is merely disorganized), and all of the aides were assigned an extra resident to care for. Mary's was Mrs. Garcia, the late Grace's roommate.

Many residents in secured units do not understand the importance of bathing and dressing. Mary was dodging blows and hearing her family curse for the next ten generations when another resident, Ethel, burst unannounced into the room.

"Help me, lady," Mrs. Garcia cried out to Ethel. "Call the police! You see that my father is forcing me to go to school this morning."

"You should be ashamed of yourself," Ethel told Mrs. Garcia.

Mrs. Garcia started to reply but didn't. Ethel was staring, transfixed, at Grace's empty bed.

"Don't you see her?" Ethel asked.

"Who?" Mary breathed. "Who do you see, Ethel?"

"Grace. She's sitting right there. Don't you see her?"

Mary felt her hair lift her scalp a centimeter off her head. In two years, she had not once heard Ethel address any resident or staff member by the correct name.

"Okay, ladies," Mary said, her breath turning to glass in her throat. "Let's go to the dining hall now." And each lady took one of Mary's hands as she quickly led them out of the room.

Later that morning, Mary made Mrs. Garcia's bed. She was alone in that room when she smelled it. Grace had been the only resident on the Sunshine Unit coherent enough to be allowed to keep perfume in her bureau. She had worn a pure rose scent, and Mary could smell it now. And this time, she was not afraid.

Mary continued to make Mrs. Garcia's bed. After a minute or so, the scent was gone.

"Goodbye, Grace," Mary whispered as she left the room.

Birth and death, Mary decided, were transitional states. Life, however, was eternal.

****

NURSING RULE # 475. In nursing school, the instructor, patient and clinical site nurses are always right, and you know nothing.

****

Stella hated Bingo Hour. She couldn't see the numbers on the damned cards, and she detested letting the solicitous volunteer help her. Besides, the Florida Forest's Bingo was not for cash.

Instead, she wandered back to her wing and told the desk nurse that she wanted to eat lunch in her room today. Idly, Stella wondered why she was called the desk nurse since she seldom could be found at the desk.

Stella wheeled into her room. Her roommate was home. She always was. Glenda Anderson was what some of the aides called a Baby Doll. They bathed her, dressed her, gave her nectar thickened juice and sang sweet lullabies to her when they thought no one else was listening. Glucerna flowed

21

from a pump through a gastric tube to Glenda's stomach. Another tube drained Glenda's urine into a catheter bag. She never spoke and rarely changed expressions.

Stella wheeled over to Glenda and smoothed the covers of her freshly made bed. Glenda smelled of shampoo and lotion. Unconsciously, Stella pushed a lock of hair out of the woman's eyes. Stella knew that she was old enough to be Glenda's mother, that the difference in their ages was enough to span a generation. But now, they were of the same age group. They were both old.

****

It was of 1995. September is the peak month of hurricane season, and 1995 was a peak hurricane year. The nursing students had nervously joked that their graduation day might be spent working as emergency relief under disaster conditions, but September 10th turned out to be a rare rainless Florida summer day.

Ellen Patrick stood in a line of starched white nursing caps. The instructors were hissing that the caps were crooked, and the first of the graduates had raced down the aisles too quickly.

The students smiled. Today would be the last day that they would have to listen to these women.

The county school administrator gave a rousing speech about the youth of America, which caused most of Ellen's class to smile politely. Ellen's adult education class was comprised more of parents of America's youth than youth itself. Still, the message was not lost on Ellen. They were students.

Looking around her, Ellen felt a surge of pride. This was her class. Some had been nurse's aides or, unit secretaries or X-ray technicians. Some had hailed from entirely different fields altogether. Most were parents. A few were grandparents. All of them had come a long way to reach this day.

They hadn't always gotten along, but they had done it together. They had survived everything from Kelly's suicide to the threatened suspension of all clinical privileges after one of them accidentally pulled out that kid's heart catheter during a routine bed bath. They had risked the wrath of the charge nurse at The Rotation from Hell by smuggling beagle puppies into the cancer unit, deciding it was better to beg forgiveness than it would have been to ask permission. And they had delivered enough socks and underwear to fill a van to their first nursing home.

The speeches were over, the candles were lit, and the nurses began receiving their pins. For some, this moment marked the end of their formal training. For others, it was a stepping stone to even higher education. For a few, it was something that they knew they would do for a while but not forever.

But for Ellen, it was the proudest moment of her life.

****

Mary was sleeping the sleep of the exhausted, the kind where you wake up for a second just to verify that you still have one or two more glorious hours of unconsciousness left when the telephone rang. Thinking it was the alarm clock, she hit the wrong button, causing rock music to flood into her room and compete with the still ringing phone. Damn! Now, who would call at this hour?

It was the night supervisor at the Florida Forest. Would Mary be able to come right in and work for a few hours?

"Oh God," she moaned. "Why do you always call me?"

"It says right here that you indicated you would be available for overtime," replied the supervisor.

"Yeah. Right. I'm sorry, I'm just tired. Okay. I'll be right in."

Mary sighed. For months now, she had been telling herself that soon she wouldn't have to do this anymore. But with two kids, a husband in prison and a job that paid just barely above minimum wage, she would have to keep on doing this.

****

"Now, Miss Vaughn, what are you doing messing around in that closet? You're going to fall."

Stella felt a flash of annoyance. Tasha was a nice girl, and she meant well, but she was also a bossy flibbertigibbet. Stella didn't suppose that it would occur to Tasha that she well knew what would and would not make her fall. That's why she had pulled her locked wheelchair behind her just so when she went to reach up to her closet shelves.

Nor did Stella wish to tell Tasha why she wanted the makeup case that Tasha had put up so high in the closet to make more room on Stella's vanity. But it was lunch time, and Tasha had to feed

Glenda, so she wasn't going to leave the room any time soon.

Stella opened the cosmetic case and began laying out her collection of pots and, tubes and brushes on the vanity. Sensing that Tasha was watching her, Stella decided to avoid being questioned by being the one asking the questions.

"Tell me something, honey," Stella said. "If she gets her food from that tube, why do you have to feed her?"

Tasha shrugged. "She doesn't eat much. The nurses call it 'pleasure food.'"

"Oh," replied Stella, opening a pot of rouge. "Well, she had to get some pleasure somewhere."

Tasha nodded, and the two fell silent. Stella streaked the bright red rouge across her cheeks, remembering a time when that had been an effortless task. Of course, then, the canvas had been smooth and unlined. Next came the sapphire blue eye shadow; her fingers were no longer nimble enough to attempt eyeliner. She then freshened her bright fuchsia lipstick.

Tasha watched silently as Stella opened a large round yellow and black box. She withdrew a powder puff and began "setting" the makeup. For a moment, Tasha almost couldn't see Stella's face for all the powder particles floating around.

"Miss Vaughn, why are you getting so dolled up?"

None of your business, Stella thought. But she smiled and replied, "I'm 103 years old. Why wait?"

****

Robert Bishop was waiting in the lobby when Stella arrived at 1:35 p.m. Stella noted that he had shaved.

They discussed what had happened at the Resident Council Meeting he had attended that morning. During the movie, he let his fingertips touch hers a few times. Stella liked the way he remained silent during Casablanca. She wondered if he, too, loved the movie or if he was just being polite.

Afterward, they went out to the West Courtyard together. Stella noticed Frances Goshen giving her dirty looks when she saw her with Robert. Well, Stella decided, Frances was a hag anyway with her rhinestones and that ridiculous dyed red hair.

Robert told her about his sons and his grandchildren and so on. And Stella told him about her life, not mentioning that she had been married five times.

Later, when she went back to her room, she didn't want to eat or talk or watch TV. She wanted to think about Robert.

Mary, the night aide, found her sitting by her open window at 3:00 a.m.

"Is anything wrong, Stella?"

Stella looked at Mary Drennan. Mary had dark circles under her eyes, but the eyes themselves were warm and compassionate. Stella could see that this was no young girl but a woman, probably a woman who had experienced love and life enough to see things from more than one perspective. Still, Stella couldn't help but wonder at how preposterous it would sound if she told Mary she couldn't sleep because she thought she was falling in love with Robert Bishop.

****

The Florida Forest had eight wings. The original structure had housed the aptly named North, South, East and West Wings. In the late 1970s, that addition that was to become the

Sunshine Unit was added on. Because the Sunshine Unit's doors opened up into a two acre fenced-in courtyard, there was no further room for expansion on the north or east sides of the building. The remaining three wings extended from the south and west sides of the structure, giving the Florida Forest a slightly lopsided appearance.

The last three wings were built in the mid-1980s. They were given lush tropical names: West Citrus Grove, Palm Acre and Tangerine Garden. The residents of these wings were low acuity, or what the nurses called the "Walkie-Talkies." These residents usually took their meals in the main dining hall of the original building, required minimal assistance with bathing and dressing and told the nurses when it was time for their medication.

The administrative and business offices were located at the center of the original structure. And at the axis of the Florida Forest began a series of suspended walkways that led to the laundry, the kitchen, Medical Records and, if you had the right key, the private apartment of Sister Mary Kate.

Sister Mary Kate was the administrator of the Florida Forest. She tolerated no deviation from what she considered to be quality care administered in a Catholic environment. She was not popular among the staff.

Sister Mary Kate was astute enough to realize that some of the nursing staff called her "Old Bat" and "Virgin Mary" behind her back. They were wrong on both counts.

Born Delores Riojas, she was only in her 40's. It was her severe black bun and stern demeanor that made her seem as if she had been born fully mature. But of course, she hadn't.

When Delores was 17, she fell in love with Kevin Foley. Soon after, he went to Vietnam. Delores thought the Vietnam War was stupid, but she didn't see the point in getting her head banged in during peace demonstrations. Instead, she spent most of the late 1960's volunteering at Catholic Charities. Keven returned home in 1970, and they were married.

On New Year's Eve of 1970, Kevin was killed in a car accident while en route from the liquor store. The champagne bottle he was bringing home to share with Delores was found on the floor of the passenger side unbroken. Kevin Foley had survived 13 months in the Vietnamese jungle only to be killed two months later, one block from his house.

Delores might have lost her mind save for the fact that she did not have that luxury. Kevin died without ever knowing what she was going to tell him that night as they toasted in the New Year with their champagne. Delores was six weeks pregnant.

The baby, a beautiful boy with hair as dark as Delores', did not survive the first week. "Crib death," the nurses whispered, something Delores had never heard of and did not understand. Her grief was like a black shroud. She sunk deeper and deeper into the layers of sorrow that enveloped and threatened to suffocate her. Finally, her parents had her placed in a mental hospital.

Delores was not crazy, and the State had no reason to keep her there. Eventually, like most wounds, Delores' healed to the point where she could function. She enrolled in the local college and studied business administration. It was almost three years after Keven's death when she made the decision to become a nun.

Sister Mary Kate did a variety of work through the years. Her job at the Florida Forest was not the first of its kind. She worked with old people, poor people, mentally challenged people and people with cancer and AIDS. The only people that Sister Mary Kate refused to work with were children. And because she was so effective at what she did do, no one in the Diocese ventured to press the issue.

In the evenings, she would return to the small living quarters and unwind with a glass of sherry. The smoke from her cigarette would drift over to the bookshelves that were overflowing with volumes of knowledge, some of it Catholic, some of it not. On the top shelf stood a bottle of champagne that had been waiting, unopened, for 25 years.

Later, she would wander into the bedroom and remove her black rimmed glasses and place them on the bureau. Then began the tedious process of removing the 30 hairpins that it took to transform her long, dark, wavy mane of hair into a tightly twisted bun.

The pins made little tinkling sounds as they hit the bureau and the bare floor. Picking up the hairbrush, she turned to the mirror and saw what few people would ever know.

Sister Mary Kate was beautiful.

****

NURSING RULE #675: The proper way to give nursing care isn't always the right way.

****

Before she became a nurse, Ellen had worked for a year as a nurse's aide. Ellen Patrick was by then nearly 31 years old. Her entire working life had been spent in offices where lifting meant carrying three reams of paper, and proper dress required shoes that kept her forever off balance. Ellen was fond of saying that the best reason to be a nurse was that the shoes were comfortable.

She had started working, at 17, as a file clerk and ended up as an office manager. Her job required her to have a mind like a computer. Endless records, systems, policies and procedures she could recall with a glance at a notation in the desk planner or the Rolodex. Ellen believed that her consistently high test scores in nursing school were owed to the fact that she had come to class already skilled at sorting large amounts of information in a short period of time.

But none of this could have prepared her for the complexities of being a nurse's aide. Waking up ten people in the morning and getting them all bathed, dressed and fed in under three hours was only half of it.

Ellen was small, weighing in at just under 120 pounds. She had, until then, spent her working life teetering around in high heels and letting the men in the office moved the boxes and the furniture. Hell, they insisted. She had yet to understand how strong her body could be.

Nurse's aides, certified under regulations of each state, are trained in the art of basic nursing. Ellen was fascinated from the start. She learned how to change the linen of a bed with the person still in it and how to transfer a person twice her size from the bed to the wheelchair. Knowing these things, somehow, empowered Ellen.

There was also much she did not know. Ellen was, quite simply, not accustomed to physical labor. By 7:30 a.m. the loose tendrils of hair that had escaped her ponytail were clinging wet against her neck. The other nurse's aides laughed at her as they saw her struggling to apply blood pressure cuff to contractured limbs and fumbling with wheelchair locks.

Ellen brought some of this on herself. It was not just her small stature and pretty blue-eyed blonde looks that made her seem like a princess. Ellen was neither naive nor simple yet there was something strikingly innocent about her that few could miss. It was this very quality that made patients intuitively trust her but it was also the same quality that made the other women laugh at her.

Ellen knew they were laughing and she knew, too, that they would not help her. And Ellen needed help. Mr. Washington was 6 feet 4 inches tall and weighed 230 pounds. He could not stand independently. The difference in their heights and the fact that he was often combative made it too perilous for Ellen to transfer him from bed to wheelchair the way she'd been taught in school. Mr. Washington was clearly a two-person lift but the other aides begged off, saying it hurt their backs to lift him.

Ellen thought they were trying to make her quit and it angered her. Actually, they weren't trying to make her quit as much as they were sure she'd never make it. Nurse's aides are generally kind and loving but they are also tough as nails. They are routinely swung at, slapped, bitten and cursed out. They are immersed daily in sights, sounds and smells that polite people do not acknowledge.

Somehow, Ellen, with her wide-eyed demeanor, did not seem to belong in their midst.

But Ellen had already decided that she was going to become a nurse.

Ellen never knew that the nurse's aides had started a betting pool on which day she would quit. But she did know that somehow she had to take care of Mr. Washington. There were a couple of aides that could be shamed into helping her and floaters from other wings might help. The houseman, if she could catch him, would help. Ellen found herself scheduling her workload around who would help her with Mr. Washington. The nurses considered it to be her problem.

One day, a floating aide from another unit showed her a trick. If she tightened her back belt and let Mr. Washington hold each of her front shoulder straps with one hand, she could then hook one arm under his armpit and grab the back of his trousers with her other hand. With one foot firmly positioned between his feet, she then had the leverage to safely lift him. It was a technique that was not written down anywhere, had not been taught in school and was probably against policy but it worked. From that day forward, Ellen knew she could lift any resident on the unit by herself.

Gradually, the other aides came to Ellen for help from time to time. She had once vowed to laugh if they ever asked her for anything but when the time came, she helped.

She tried to teach the other aides how she managed to lift Mr. Washington by herself but it was no use. Ellen was the only one who could coax him to hold on to the shoulder straps of her back belt. They continued to have a rough time with Mr. Washington on Ellen's days off.

Although the nurse's aides had angered her in the beginning, nothing pleased her more than their eventual acceptance of her as one of their own. Ellen was proud to be one of them. They could detect changes in a resident's condition long before the nurses could. They could convince combative and demented to let them assist with the most private and personal aspects of life. They could calm agitated residents with no more than one well-chosen word or phrase. The realm was one that medicine could never touch.

****

NURSING RULE #747: The higher up you go in your nursing career, the further away you get from your patients.

****

Robert Bishop sighed in annoyance. He had been floating in a comfortable cloud of sleep when the familiar urgency woke him up. It wasn't that he minded having to get up to take a leak as much as he minded the fact that once he got to the bathroom, he might find he couldn't go after all. But the urgency was terrible and he couldn't just lay there.

Robert sat on the edge of the bed, taking the time to put on his skid-proof slippers. More than one fellow Robert knew had gotten up in the middle of the night to take a leak and had slipped and broken a hip. The hall lights were soft at this hour and water, pee, or anything else could be on the floor. You just never knew.

Of course, he could have called for the night aide, but Robert Bishop firmly believed that the day he couldn't take a leak by himself was the day he'd better die.

Once he got there, it took him a while to urinate. It was uncomfortable, too. Enlarged prostate, the doctor said, and prescribed little blue pills. Lately, though, they didn't seem to be working.

Back in bed now, he found that he was fully awake. That Stella Vaughn was something else. Robert smiled. He'd heard that she'd been married five times. People said this as if there was something loose or disagreeable about her, but Robert could only wonder at the charm and beauty that had captivated five men into asking for her hand and the boundless energy and faith she must have had to have accepted five times.

Idly, he wondered how old she was. Probably about 80 or so.

Just as he was about to drift off into sleep again, he felt the urge to take another leak. He was not going to get up again. There was no way his bladder could have filled in that short of a time. As he closed his eyes, he made a mental note to speak with the nurse in the morning.

****

Ellen had been the night nurse for a month now. She no longer knew day from night nor cared about such distinctions.

Ellen was in charge of Three South from 7:00 p.m. until 7:00 a.m. Forty residents were under her care and at least 15 of them were given to night wandering. As she passed medications, flushed Gtubes and changed catheters, Ellen often wondered at the miracle that always matched the right procedure with the right patient. Or so she prayed.

The night supervisor wasn't much help. She considered the position to be a windfall for a new nurse and was surprised that Ellen didn't seem more grateful.

Making sure that the nurse's aides had everyone properly turned and positioned was Ellen's responsibility, as was being certain that water pitches were always fresh, full and within reach. She was responsible for ensuring that the laundry brought up enough linen and that housekeeping took care of all spills. Seeing to it that all residents who went to first breakfast were up and dressed by the end of her shift was her responsibility. Ensuring that all labs were drawn on time was her responsibility. Everything, Ellen decided, must be her responsibility.

All of this sudden responsibility, coupled with the weird way that night shift work tampers with the body's primitive circadian rhythm, made Ellen very cranky with her staff, but she was not unfair. She would stop her own work to help any aide who needed her. She would also send packing any aide who didn't have the inclination to perform basic nursing care.

The day shift nurses were under the impression that Ellen had nothing to do at night, which added to her frustration. But no matter how tired or irritated she felt, she never let her residents know. At times, she felt like crying, but instead, she gave her sunny smile, soothing voice and gentle touch to those entrusted in her care. And that quality, more than all of the clinical and technical knowledge in the world, is what separates the real nurse from someone who simply holds a valid nursing license.

****

The phone range deep inside the private chambers of Sister Mary Kate. It was the Bishop Adams. When the phone conversation was finished, there was nothing to indicate that Sister Mary Kate was shaken. She went about her duties for the rest of the day, her secret betrayed neither by word or deed. Sister Mary Kate hated being the very first to know something that would greatly impact hundreds of people in a short time.

Day blended into evening and she drifted back to her apartment. It was the hour after sunset and the Florida Forest buzzed with an energy of its own. The drone of the television sets, the clinking of the silver, the sweet smell from the still warm linen. These were the scents and sounds of a well-oiled, neatly run facility. Sister Mary Kate sighed.

The Activities Department was setting up for the country/western band. Some of the residents, including Robert Bishop and Stella Vaughn, had arrived early. Mary Drennan, working the first half of a double shift, had styled Stella's hair into a side sweep for the occasion, securing it with a large comb. It seemed a little too sophisticated for her casual outfit, but Stella didn't mind. Mary was a sweet gal and, at 103, Stella was thankful she still had hair.

Robert Bishop smelled like Old Spice and Mineral Ice. His back was sore but he wanted nothing to interfere with this evening with Stella. Besides, he was sure it was nothing more than plain old age.

In the main dayroom, residents argued over the news on television. Aides passed fruit juices and watched for warning signs of falls, fisticuffs or anything else that might generate an Incident Report. On the South Wing a new nurse named Ellen prayed for the strength to survive this night.

Meanwhile, on East Wing a resident named Dolly, with beautiful hair and bright coal-black eyes told her aide that she would not survive the night. She did this by taking Mary's hand in her own diminutive one and saying "Goodbye, honey. I'm going home now."

Mary knew what that meant. Mary told Susan, the evening nurse. Susan was annoyed to find Dolly calm and pleasant with perfectly stable vital signs. "I've never felt finer," she told Susan.

And Susan told Mary in so many words that Mary didn't know what she was talking about, but Mary didn't care what Susan thought.

In West Citrus Grove Frances Goshen fretted the loss of her top dentures. West Citrus Grove was a low-acuity unit. No wanderers lived there but there was nothing stopping them from wandering in and taking other resident's belongings. Frances knew they couldn't help it, knew that for the grace of God she could be wandering and muttering and pilfering, but still. There should be some way to stop it.

It was probably a good thing that no one had seen Stella Vaughn enter Frances Goshen's room shortly after Stella had seen Frances flirting with Robert Bishop.

Later that night on North Wing, Robert Bishop once again awoke needing to take a leak. This time it took forever, and he noticed that the stream seemed thinner. The day nurse had already made an appointment for him to see a urologist.

Very late into the night, Dolly died while Mary held her hand.

And no one anywhere in the Florida Forest knew what Sister Mary Kate knew. The Catholic Diocese was selling the Florida Forest to a private healthcare management company.

It was not for herself that Sister Mary Kate was upset. She was a servant of the Lord, and she went wherever the Diocese sent her. And this was hardly the first time that such a thing had happened. Managed care was slowly edging the churches out of the health care industry. But this time, it hurt.

Sister Mary Kate was familiar with the company that would buy the Florida Forest. They were most notable for high-profit margins and least notable for quality patient care. When the Church left, life would irrevocably change for 500 vulnerable residents.

And for the first time since the death of Kevin Foley, Delores Riojas began to cry.

NURSING RULE #847: Nurses are required to know a lot about medicine but doctors aren't required to know a thing about nursing.

The Florida Forest was overrun with stray cats. So many of the residents left little cereal bowls of milk outside the place that some of the cats grew fat and seemed to lose their scavenging instincts.

To Ellen, they were a nuisance. Every time she got out of her car, it seemed, one would jump on the hood and hiss at her.

"Shoo!" she hissed back. "Bad enough you drink all their milk. Now you have to act like you own the place too!" The tabby, a green-eyed calico beauty, stared coolly at Ellen.

On the way in Ellen said a pleasant hello to Joe; the young resident danced to what the nurses called the "Huntington's Dance." Huntington's disease is a disorder of the central nervous system that results in involuntary and sometimes bizarre movements. The wonder was not that Joe fell down

45

as often as he did but that he didn't do it more often. Still, it didn't seem right to confine him to a wheelchair or bed. That would happen soon enough on its own.

At change of shift, Ellen learned she had a new resident. Phillip Johnson, 28 years old, was admitted for wasting syndrome secondary to AIDS. Ellen's expression never changed, but the color temporarily left her face.

Few nurses will admit they are afraid to care for AIDS patients; to do so is career suicide. Nurses are supposed to know that HIV is not spread through casual contact. But much of the contact between nurses and patients is not casual.

Ellen had more than her own fears to deal with. The confidentiality factor was like a bomb ready to blow up in her face, but the nursing staff needed to know. Some of the aides were frightened. Ellen found herself repeating the ways that HIV can be transmitted: Blood, semen and vaginal fluid. The information didn't seem to help much.

By early morning, it was apparent that the ancillary personnel like laundry and housekeeping, also knew the diagnosis of her newest resident. Ellen knew there would be hell to pay. Ancillary personnel were not directly involved in resident care and had no legal right to know. Yet, they were almost as likely as the nursing staff to encounter body fluids in the course of their work. Again, Ellen repeated the ways in which HIV is transmitted.

Phillip Johnson was a quiet and gentle man who didn't seem to want to bother anybody. Sometimes, when he was too weak to walk, Ellen would wheel him out to the porch so he could smoke his Kools. He never asked for anything more.

One evening at shift change, Ellen found Phillip talking out of his head. "AIDS dementia," the more experienced day nurse told her. His blood pressure was 80/40, temperature 103.6 F, pulse 122 and thready, respirations 44.

"AIDS dementia, my ass," Ellen replied. "He's dying."

"Ellen," the day nurse replied gently. "These people run night fevers. It's not uncommon." But Ellen was not convinced. His lips were blue, and his nail beds were dusky. Hadn't the nurse noticed?

Phillip had kicked off the blankets and was thrashing around on the bed. Ellen was experienced enough to know that he needed oxygen and that she didn't have time to get a doctor's order. She grabbed the green canister from the crash cart and set the flowmeter at 3 liters per minute. Then she called the doctor.

Twenty minutes later, the nurse practitioner called her back. "Give him oxygen at 3 liters per minute and 1 cc of morphine every two hours as needed. And, ah, yeah .... We'll need a CBC and a SMAC 7."

It was the moment Ellen had dreaded since Phillip's arrival to the unit. She was going to risk her life by accessing his bloodstream.

It's no riskier than driving, she told herself, and I do that every day. No riskier than facing agitated patients who could strangle her. No riskier than walking these halls where she could slip on urine and break her neck.

"Phillip," she gently nudged. "Phillip, wake up, darling. I've got to get some blood." Phillip had been asleep since almost the precise moment when she had placed the oxygen cannula under his nostrils.

Ellen grabbed the tourniquet. His arms were so pitifully thin and mottled and he looked so tired that she hated to bother him.

"I'm so sorry to bother you," she said as she applied the tourniquet and prepped the skin.

"That's okay," he replied weakly. "You've been real nice to me."

"Well Phil, whatever you do please don't move. If I get stuck with this needle, I'm going to be as sick as you are."

"Oh no," he groaned. "I don't want anybody to be this sick."

And Phillip did not move. And Ellen did a perfect blood draw, accessing the vein on the first try. The blood flowed back into the vial, looking just like any other blood she had ever seen. As Ellen placed the vial in the lab sleeve, she felt her knees turn to water. The vial contained one of the most lethal viruses in the history of the world.

Later that night, Phillip began vomiting mercilessly. Again, Ellen risked contact that was far from casual. She drew up 5mg of Compazine in a syringe and placed the needle in the upper outer quadrant above the buttocks. It was the gluteus medius and the only place left on Philllip's body with enough flesh to make an intramuscular injection feasible.

Phillips nausea subsided, and Ellen forgot about him for a while as she tended to her other 39 residents.

"It must be a full moon," Mary Drennan remarked as she opened the linen closet door. Ellen nodded.

Mrs. Antoniak was about to, without provocation, pinch Mrs. Hawkins. Rose, the night aide, intercepted, causing Mrs. Antoniak to pinch Rose instead. Mr. Stans was angry because Mrs. Jones was using his bathroom. And unbeknownst to Mary, Mrs. Cates had just walked off with a stack of washcloths.

Sometimes, Ellen took a moment to listen to the sounds that were her unit.

"Bo-bo-bo-bo-bo-bo."

"Oh, shut up!"

"Why there ain't no fish in that pond. If there was, I would have seen them."

"Hey, hey, hey, hey."

"Get away from me! If I'd been able to impregnate myself, I'd never have had anything to do with a man at all!"

"No, I'm going home! My children are there, and they need me."

Ellen snapped to attention at this last. It was Mrs. Donovan, one of South Wing's night wanderers. If Ellen knew nothing else, she knew this: crazy or sane, if a woman believes her children need her no one is going to talk her out of trying to leave. Ellen called the Sunshine Unit to alert them that she might have to temporarily place Mrs. Donovan for the night.

Phillips family came in later that evening. His mother sought Ellen out. Ellen had no words for this woman who was losing her youngest son, but she listened. And sometimes that is enough.

Mrs. Donovan was placed on the Sunshine Unit after Rose found her in a resident's room, trying to climb out of the window.

Later, Phillip began having violent diarrhea. Ellen procured a bedside commode, but he must have forgotten because she found him lying on the bathroom floor.

"I fell," he said. And after checking for blood (there was none), Ellen gently lifted the emaciated man and helped him back to bed. She replaced the oxygen cannula.

"It's all my own stupid fault," Phillip moaned.

"What is?"

"All of this. Being sick."

"How did you get AIDS, Phil?"

"Needles. Drugs. I was a dumb ass."

Ellen felt angry. No one should have to pay this price for a mistake. She didn't know what to say so she took his hand. He fell asleep again.

Later, Rose called her. "Can you give him something more for diarrhea? It's bad."

Ellen nodded, filled a medicine cup, and went into Phillip's room. He could no longer make it to the bedside commode. She filled a basin with water and carried it to Phillip's bed.

"Phil, honey. I'm going to help you clean up a little."

Phillip nodded without opening his eyes. Ellen drew the curtains around the bed and lifted the sheet, her nurse's eyes automatically assessing his stool for color and consistency.

What she saw would haunt her for the rest of her life. But it was too late to turn back now. It had been too late since that day in the insurance office, surrounded by colored paper clips and sticky memo notes, when she had decided to become a nurse.

Ellen really didn't know much more about HIV infection than the average person who is in the habit of reading the daily newspaper. And she was no less afraid of an incurable fatal virus than anyone else. But she was the nurse.

And so it was Ellen who cleaned him that night, Ellen who fed him morphine and Ellen who gently injected Compazine.

The air in Phillip's room seemed rarified, and the light over his bed appeared to glow with a golden, rosy light. The soft evening breeze through the open window smelled of orange blossoms, their scent sweeter than Ellen could ever remember.

Mary Drennan whispered to Ellen that the angels were in Phillip's room. Ellen nodded.

"Monica!" Phillip cried out. "Don't leave me!"

"I won't, darling," Ellen answered. "I'm right here." Ellen would be Monica if it would make Phillip's last hours easier. Nurses have become wives, sweethearts, mothers and children during the hours that the angels gather.

"I'm so sorry this happened. I love you, Monica."

"I love you too, Phil."

And it was in Ellen's arms, hearing the forgiving voice of Monica, that Phillip Johnson died at 4:07 a.m.

****

Across town, at the Rose Forest Home for the Aged, Mildred Stapleton was getting dressed. She was trying to tie her plum-colored scarf around her neck when she heard a knock on the door.

"Come in."

It was Maria, her aide. "Happy Birthday, Mrs. Stapleton."

"Thank you, honey. Tell me, does this scarf go with my dress?"

Maria shook her head. "Not really. The yellow would be better."

Mildred looked doubtful for a moment and then acquiesced. "Okay, you win. I know you've got taste."

"What are you going to do for your birthday, Mrs. Stapleton?"

"My mother is coming to see me."

A look of concern crossed Maria's face. She'd never known Mrs. Stapleton to be confused before.

"Your mother?"

"Yes. She lives across town. Doesn't get out much."

I imagine not, Maria thought. She told the nurse about Mrs. Stapleton's confusion.

"I mean, she's 87, and I've never heard her talk about her mother before. I'm sure her mom's dead. She's 87."

The nurse nodded. "Get me some vital signs, and I'll order lab work. Keep an eye on her."

Maria nodded and took the Dina Map to Mildred's room.

"Hi again, Mrs. Stapleton. I'm going to take your blood pressure and your temperature."

'Okay, but I don't know what for. I made it this far, didn't I? .... Oh, hi Mom!"

Maria turned to see Stella Vaughn.

****

PART TWO

Mildred Stapleton was Stella's oldest child. Stella had been only 16 and wildly in love with Johnny Richards, who became her first husband. John was a drunk and a cheater but Stella adored him and it broke her heart when he left her and the baby for Harriet Simpson, a busty blonde who wore gold heart jewelry in every place a woman could wear jewelry (at least in those days.)

Not that finding another man in her tiny Indiana town would have been difficult, not even with her infant daughter and her not quite pretty face. Stella Richards had an unaffected, vivacious energy that few could miss and none could touch. She had a way of tossing her honey colored halo of hair and smiling that was neither calculated nor flirtatious but nonetheless managed to entrance every male who ever saw it. Yet she was so warm and candid that most women liked her too.

Furthermore, Stella owned a pair of long, lovely voluptuous legs. Stella had always reasoned that her face was so plain because God must have figured that her legs were gift enough.

"Funny face," the men called her, right to her face. Behind her back, they said, "Legs clean up to her neck. She could wrap those around you twice." Even with the long skirts of that day they could see that.

The women said things behind her back too. "Poor thing. Her husband left her and her baby for a tramp just because she wasn't pretty enough." To her face, they said, "You're better off without him, dear."

Stella supposed they were right, but she still missed Johnny. She never felt any bitterness, just sorrow.

Stella went on to marry four more times in her life and she was to bear seven children. All of her husbands had passed away by now, although two of them died years after divorce and remarriage to either women. Thus, Stella had been a widow three times.

The last time had been fairly recent. John Vaughn had passed peacefully in his sleep four months after the wedding that had made the news from coast to coast. The 98-year-old groom and his 101 year old bride. After John's death Stella moved into the Florida Forest because she didn't want to live alone ever again.

Of all of her marriages, Stella had gone into her last knowing that their time together would be brief. But of all of her husbands, she missed John Vaughn the most.

Even more than John, she missed her children. It has been said that to lose a child is to know life's greatest tragedy but to Stella, who had lost five, it was more than tragic. It was unnatural.

Charlie, her youngest, had died first, in a blast of gunfire outside of a Chicago speakeasy, the implications of which were lost on his small-town Indiana mother. Then Hazel died in childbirth. The other three; Harry, William and Louise, succumbed in their 70's and 80's to the old age betrayals of heart attack and stroke. Rosemary had not been as lucky, Stella thought. Her stroke had left her voiceless and motionless but not lifeless. Only her Mildred was doing well. She was 87 and living in an old folk's home.

The deaths of Charlie and Hazel had crushed Stella but the deaths of her other children had done something else. They had made Stella think that she had lived too long.

Why had the good Lord, in His infinite wisdom, let her live so long? Stella couldn't help but wonder. Why had He allowed her heart to continue on with its lub-dub, every eight-tenths of a second without fail for 103 years while the hearts of almost everyone else she had ever loved had been stilled?

Sometimes Stella thought that perhaps God had forgotten about her, that she should have been called years ago but somehow her file had gotten lost on some heavenly desk. Or perhaps it was in some huge electronic data base and because she'd had so many married names, the computer could no longer accommodate her, and her file was lost forever in divine cyberspace.

And now there was Robert Bishop. Stella closed her eyes against the pain of remembering John's death. She could not go through it again, she would not. Nor could she put Robert through it.

Stella was 103, and Robert was 92. They could not possibly have much time together.

And yet it was not far beneath her time-worn skin nor far removed from her age old wisdom that 16-year old Stella Richards still lived. She would forever be that long-legged, honey-haired girl whose plain face became lovely whenever she saw life's endless possibilities for beauty and wonder bound toward her.

****

NURSING TIP#1: Never tell a confused patient that you are going to take his or her vitals.

****

It was 6:30 p.m. when Ellen arrived in the locker room. The official shift change was 6:45, but most nurses arrived earlier than that. Ellen enjoyed the time before the shift change. It gave both shifts a chance to exchange gossip and patient information. This information often proved to be more accurate than what they learned in meetings and at official shift change reports.

"Who's bring the coffee?"

"I am. Here. Hazelnut or French Vanilla?"

"Christ, whatever happened to just regular coffee?"

"Don't bitch. You aren't paying for it."

"And neither are you."

"Well, with all the double shifts we've been working, it's not like we couldn't pay for it."

"How's Mrs. Monroe?"

"Lord, she went on and on all day like she was on a drunken binge. You should see her labs. Her electrolytes are all out of whack."

"What'd the doctor do?"

"Ordered more lab work."

"Jesus."

"That's nothing. You know how they had Mrs. Kinkaid on three different antibiotics? Now I ask you, what kind of urinary tract infection does she have that she needs three different antibiotics? Well, her stool is bad. I mean really bad. And you would not believe what I had to go through to get an order to test her for C.difficile. Why, the great doctor wants to know, do you want to test her for C.diff? 'Because," I said. 'She's on three different antibiotics and she can't stay off the toilet.' And do you know what he asked me?"

"What?"

"Why is she on three different antibiotics?' "

"Good God."

"Uh-huh. People think we make this stuff up."

"Hey, who's smoking?"

"Me."

"Put it out."

"Why?"

"Cause you're not supposed to smoke in her, that's why."

"Why not? The residents smoke inside."

"They live here."

"Shit. With all of these double shifts we live here."

"Quit complaining. You don't have to work doubles."

"If Virgin Mary catches you smoking in here you are fired."

"Who cares? The Old Bat is on her way out. Haven't you heard?"

"No. What?"

"They're selling this place."

"No way. To who?"

"The same folks that bought Rose Forest two years ago.

"No!" They were awful. They almost ruined that place."

"Well, it's better there now."

"Yeah after the State almost shut them down."

"Oh stop it. Rose Forest had a lot of problems before they were sold. What happened there could never happen here. I mean, we wouldn't let it. We wouldn't let it and neither would our residents."

"That's right."

"Damned straight."

Susan, who had been standing next to Ellen, slammed her locker shut so suddenly that Ellen, who had been listening intently to the other nurses, jumped.

"Couldn't happen here, huh?" Susan asked no one in particular. "What do you think you're going to do when your residents have bedsores to the bone because you don't have enough aides to care for them? And the State inspectors are all over you because the wounds don't heal? The wounds don't heal because suddenly you don't have really basic stuff like zinc and Vitamin C. Medicaid doesn't pay for vitamins and minerals, the facility does. Only now, they don't. Not anymore. Now they're making a profit by giving themselves a pay raise. Which they pay for by eliminating your job because you can't heal the wounds and you make them look bad to the State. You think I'm kidding? I was at Rose Forest when those assholes took over."

No one answered Susan. It was 6:45. Ellen gently closed her locker and set the combination. Ellen didn't know if Susan was right or not and right now, she didn't care. It was going to take everything she had just to get through this night with the Florida Forest the way it was now.

****

NURSING TIP #2: You are not, nor will you ever be, Florence Nightingale.

****

One of the first acts of the new administration of the Florida Forest was to reorganize the staff that had not been eliminated. Ellen was not only organized to another wing but to another shift.

Ellen quickly learned the difference between having forty residents under her care at night and having the same number on the day shift. The old administration has assigned two medication nurses per wing on the day shift but this day found Ellen working the North Wing alone.

Ellen was looking for something to mix her crushed meds in. She hated using applesauce. Most residents disliked the combination, and a few would spit the bitter mixture back at her. Ice cream melted too fast to be useful. Pudding was good, but the new administration said it was too expensive and forbade its use on the med cart. Finally, she grabbed a few jelly packets from the unit kitchen. Jelly was hard to use because you often ended up with a red or purple ball that wouldn't quite pick up all of the medication particles in the cup, but it was better than nothing. Taking a deep breath and checking the clock on the wall, she began her morning medication pass.

Room 102 was a private room, as were all of the front hall rooms nearest the nurses' station. People lucky enough to afford private rooms had no roommates to alert the staff when sickness came quickly.

The occupant of Room 102 was a large woman with a commanding presence. She didn't know Ellen, but Ellen knew her. Everyone at the Florida Forest had heard of Miss Florence, an aging socialite who was reputed to be demanding and rude.

"Who are you?" Miss Florence asked suspiciously.

"My name is Ellen Patrick. I'm your nurse."

"You're not my nurse. My nurse is Patty. I've never seen you before."

"I used to work nights on South Wing."

"Well, what riffraff are they sending us now? How old are you? Seventeen?"

"I'm 33."

"Yeah and I'm 25. I need you to take my breakfast tray."

The tray cart, Ellen knew, was on the far end of the opposite hall. The aides were picking up the trays. They'd get to Miss Florence in about five minutes."

"Can you wait five minutes for the aides to pick it up?

"No, I need it taken away now. That's what I pay you for."

"No problem," Ellen replied sweetly. It was no problem at all to walk down both halls to place a tray on a cart when she had over 200 medications to pass in less than two hours.

"I need you to bring me a towel and a washcloth."

Ellen knew that the fresh laundry hadn't arrived yet. First delivery was due in about five minutes.

"The aides will be bringing the towels right after they pick up the trays," Ellen promised.

"Well, the aides do everything don't they? And just what is it that you do?"

"I bring you your medicine. Here."

"Well, you have the easy job, don't you?"

"Yes ma'am," Ellen replied evenly. "It's a snap."

Miss Florence gazed at Ellen for a moment. "You're skinny," she observed.

And you're fat, Ellen answered silently as she picked up the empty medicine cup and Miss Florence's breakfast tray.

Ellen was thinking that Miss Florence was a rude old woman. Miss Florence was thinking that Ellen was a snippy young woman. And neither woman realized that in less than six months Miss Florence would die with Ellen holding her hand.

The next room promised to be easier. Lilly and Rose were both diagnosed as schizophrenic. They lived in nervous, anxious, private worlds. Both women received their medication and nutrition through gastric tubes. Ellen worked rapidly, the Silent Knight transforming pills into powder fine enough to dissolve completely in water before being poured into a 60cc syringe. She added water to the cups and stirred the pale pastel fluids. Next came the elixirs, red and purple syrups that gleamed like dark jewels next to the pink, yellow and mint green water. Lastly, she prepared the potassium, using a larger cup to ensure that the potent mineral was fully diluted. The result resembled weak orange Kool-Aid.

"Pretty," observed a blue-haired lady. "Can I have one?"

"No ma'am. They're medicine."

"Oh," the woman replied. "Well, I hope you know what you're doing."

Ellen grinned as she entered Room 104. Lilly reminded Ellen of a little girl despite her obvious evidence of age. She had a soft, almost spooky voice, luminous blue eyes and wispy white hair. She disliked having her gastric tube flushed and it was only the constant steady drone of her nurses' voices that got her through the procedure without sheer hysteria. Ellen soothed and stroked. Lilly had a piece of Ellen's smock in each of her small fists.

"It's almost over, Miss Lilly, it's almost over."

Ellen felt rather than heard someone enter the room. It was Mrs. Brennan, the Florida Forest's oldest resident. At 106, Mrs. Brennan spent her days wandering from wing to wing in her wheelchair, stealing other resident's belongings.

An oversized Raggedy Ann doll belonging to Rose caught Mrs. Brennan's fancy, and she snatched it as Rose screamed in protest. Ellen tried to loosen Lilly's grip on her smock and was rewarded as Lilly snatched her bandage scissors out of her pocket. Ellen retrieved the scissors and then the Raggedy Ann, but not without Mr. Brennan slapping Ellen's arms and scolding her. Rose sobbed loudly until Ellen hugged and kissed her.

Quickly now, Ellen returned to her med pass. She poured the liquids down Lilly's tube, hardly feeling the small, angry old fingers pinching in protest as she talked Lilly through the post-med flush. Next, she hung a fresh bag of Osmolite, changed the tubing and was halfway through with priming the tubing when she heard it.

"NURSE!!!"

For the briefest fraction of a second Ellen froze and then she sprang like a deer into action. Quickly, so quickly, she remembered to turn off Lilly's tube feeding so she would not return to the room later to find an Incident Report generated over a puddle of slippery Osmolite on the floor. Almost simultaneously, she was at Tasha's side.

"What's wrong with her?" Tasha cried.

It was Stephanie, a resident no older than Tasha. Stephanie's boyfriend had choked Stephanie not to death but into a vegetative state. She had been at the Florida Forest for four days, days in which Tasha had talked to her and played the radio for her while she combed and braided her hair. Now Stephanie looked as if the last traces of life had been erased from her young face and she was moaning. Her respirations were wet and gurgling.

"I need to suction her," Ellen said, and Tasha moved to the opposite side of the bed to hold Stephanie's hand.

Almost immediately, Ellen brought up bright red blood clots. She cut the power to the suction machine and told Tasha, "Stay with her. I'm going to send her to the Emergency Room."

Tasha nodded, fighting back tears.

Ellen made the calls, to the doctor, the emergency medical facility and the family. There was no answer at Stephanie's mother's house. Ellen rapidly filled out the forms and made copies. Paperwork. There was always paperwork at a time like this.

Ellen cursed the triplicate forms, all six of them, but she completed them in their entirety. To send Stephanie to the Emergency Room without properly completed paperwork would almost certainly delay her care.

The paramedics arrived at the same time as Stephanie's mother, who had dropped by to visit her daughter on her way to work. Ellen directed the paramedics to Stephanie's room and answered their questions. No sooner had they placed the young woman on the stretcher when she had a convulsive seizure.

Stephanie was coded; once, twice, three times but she died right there with five medical personnel in vain attendance as the bright morning sun washed Room 110 with light.

And the heart of Stephanie's mother broke in that room. Tasha could hear it in her agonized wail. The woman collapsed on Tasha's breast, and Tasha embraced her, their tears mingling into a single flow.

Ellen was relieved that Tasha could handle Stephanie's mother for the moment. She would have to complete more paperwork to ensure the removal of Stephanie's body from the facility in a timely and dignified manner. And she still had nearly forty residents who were still waiting for their morning medicine.

****

NURSING TIP #3: A little cranberry juice will dissolve most matter that clogs a G-tube. Just be sure to flush with 120 cc of water for every one ounce of juice.

****

Carmen Manriquez was a middle aged woman although she resembled a little girl. Constant repetitive pacing up and down the wing kept her body small and thin. The aides had long ago learned that it was better to hand Carmen her pureed meal in a cup with a spoon and let her walk around the wing while she ate than it would have been to get her to sit down at a table with the other residents.

Carmen had an inexplicable attachment to blankets. She would snatch them from other residents and become agitated if anyone intervened. She rarely made eye contact with other people, seemingly oblivious to the world outside of herself. She rarely spoke, and when she did, it made no sense to anyone else.

Mary was an aide and not a nurse and therefore she wasn't allowed to access resident's medical records. Mary was not exactly sure what Carmen's diagnosis was. Most of the aides said she was autistic, but Mary wasn't sure. In all of her years of working as an aide, Mary had never met anyone exactly like Carmen.

While Mary didn't know exactly what Carmen's diagnosis was, she did understand that Carmen was a savant. Carmen could draw anything she had ever seen. Mary discovered this one day when she found Carmen working on a drawing. It was a drawing of Mary, and Mary gasped in astonishment when she saw it. It was like looking into a mirror.

After that Mary spent extra time with Carmen, trying to make contact with her, if only for just a moment. If Carmen noticed, she never let it show.

Looking through the window, Ellen could see Mary in the courtyard with Carmen, handing her a snack in a cup with a spoon. Carmen never looked up but she must have known it was there because she took it. And a few moments later she tossed the cup into the azalea bush.

Mary went to retrieve the cup, and by the time she got their, Carmen was busily tearing the leaves off of the bush. Mary intervened, an act that would normally have set off a tantrum, but Carmen merely handed Mary a pink blossom.

"Did you see that?" Ellen asked Susan, who had come over from East Wing to see if Ellen had any zinc oxide on her cart. "If that had been anybody but Mary, she would have screamed for an hour. Mary is amazing. She can get through to people when no one else can. I wonder why she never became a nurse?"

"She's probably too smart to do something that stupid," Susan replied.

****

NURSING TIP #4: Don't use applesauce to mix crushed meds in. It tastes terrible.

****

Dr. Johnson looked grim. He placed Robert's open chart on the exam table. From his chair, Robert could see words like neoplasm and metastasis. These were words Robert had seen before. These were words, he knew, that told the tale of a single cell gone wild.

"This is most unusual," Dr. Johnson was saying as he showed Robert X-rays of the cancer from his prostate, now living deep in his lumbar vertebrae, his pelvis and his hips.

"Most unusual and most disturbing," Dr. Johnson continued. "Your last PSA was within normal limits and prostate cancer generally takes years to grow like this. This is nearly unprecedented, in my experience."

Robert didn't answer. What was he supposed to say? He had no doubt that the doctor was correct. The pain in his back and hips was becoming hard to bear, but the pain that had shot down his leg earlier that morning had nearly felled him.

The doctor was talking about something called palliative radiation for the pain. Robert said that he wanted to think about it first. He thanked the doctor and left.

On the way back he talked and joked with the driver of the Florida Forest bus. The driver was going to go away for the weekend to a family reunion in George with five generations under one picnic awning.

"Oh, I'm glad you're back from the doctor's office, Mr. Bishop," the nurse greeted him. "I still have to give you your heart pill." And as the nurse listened to Robert's heartbeat through her hot pink stethoscope, he stared at the small yellow pill in the white paper cup in her hand as if he had never seen it before.

Marion, his wife of 50 years, had died of breast cancer. He remembered how she fought, how her complexion had gone from rosy to white to yellow to gray. He remembered how she had cried out in pain, how that odor lingered in the room months after her death. The room in which Robert never again slept.

Robert knew that cancer therapy had greatly improved in the 20 years since Marion's death knew that the external beam radiation that Dr. Johnson had spoken of was nothing at all like the hideous cobalt treatments of the past. But still, facts were facts. And the fact was, Robert Bishop was 93 years old.

He was not going to fight for his life.

And as he raised the pill cup to his lips, he began to formulate a plan.

****

NURSING TIP#5: Use an alcohol swab when removing adhesive bandages from hairy body parts. Your patients will thank you for it.

****

"Mrs. Vaughn, I cannot be silent any longer," Robert Bishop said. "I am falling in love with you."

"Well, that being the case, don't you think you ought to call me 'Stella'?"

Robert didn't answer. He knew that Stella wasn't really answering him. The two sat in silence a little longer watching the red and orange hibiscus blossom retract against the impeding twilight. Somewhere in the distance, a single frog croaked again and again, its lone voice filling acres of the Florida Forest.

"Amazing how one frog can make such a racket, isn't it?" Stella asked.

Robert's nod was barely perceptible. He was too old to be impatient but plenty old enough to be stubborn. Stella would answer him when she was good and ready and not a moment before. In the meantime, he would not answer her.

And so, Stella talked awhile among the cricket symphony that gradually matched the croaking of the frog.

"Listen, Robert," she said. "The birds, the crickets, all of them are talking but soon ...... and all at once .... they will hush. The night will fall. They know that there's a time and a place for everything.

"Even that frog," she went on. "Even he knows when his hour of glory is over."

And Robert said nothing. And finally, when night fell and the animal sounds were halted, Stella answered him.

"It won't work, Robert."

"Why not?"

Stella again felt the crush of pain that was John Vaughn's death. She turned to Robert and looked straight into his bright blue eyes.

"Because it is very likely that one of us will die soon. Or worse, after a while when we've gotten used to having each other."

"Stella," Robert said, taking her hands in his. "We're going to die soon anyway."

And Stella knew that Robert had a point. Perhaps this cricket filled evening was all there ever was, all that had ever really existed.

Stella looked down at their entwined hands. Robert's were long and pale with tens of liver spots. Her own reminded her of the tissue paper she had used .... oh so many years ago ...... to make paper flowers attached to pipe cleaners stems, gifts for her mother and her aunts.

The four ancient hands together seemed to form a synergy born of their combined nearly two hundred years of life, a power greater than their frail bodies would sustain.

Critical mass was reached when Stella smiled at Robert. The energy broke apart, going back through the years so that their time on earth was no longer long enough to be powerful.

Stella stood up out of her wheelchair and tossed her walker aside. She no longer needed either one. Robert and Stella were no longer old. They were middle-aged, in that delicious wine sap time of life when the bloom of youth is gone, but old age has yet to arrive.

Robert was quite striking. Tall and well-groomed, he cut a distinguished figure as the two of them walked hand in hand through this time. Middle age had alighted on Stella with the exquisite grace that is a gift given only to those who were plain-faced in youth. Her legs were strong and lovely again. She held her tall carriage proudly as she walked with Robert through the brightly colored red, gold and orange foliage. She knew people were looking at them. They were a handsome couple. As she breathed in the crisp fall air and felt the golden autumn sunshine on her face, Stella thought that she would never wish for anything more in life ever again.

And now, they were in a meadow, and it was much warmer. It was summer! Robert and Stella removed their suit jackets and their shoes and stockings. They were young again. Stella was astounded at the rugged masculine beauty of Robert's coal black hair against bright blue eyes paired with a long, strong body. Her own honey colored hair fell in soft natural waves against her face and shoulders again. She tossed it back and laughed, entrancing Robert with the way her plain face was transformed when her dark emerald eyes lit up.

It was full summer in the meadow. Butterflies and wildflowers and clover and honeybees surrounded them. Robert placed a chain of daisies on Stella's hair like a crown.

They both stripped down to golden skin, their young bodies not unlike Greek sculptures in the sunlight. They were both so tall and graceful that the vision of their embrace was enough to still the sounds of the birds and the insects for one awed moment.

The first man, the first woman. And they found a place to be alone in that meadow.

And now, they were standing by a babbling brook. They tested the water with their toes and found it chilly. It was springtime, and mud squished beneath their bare feet. The first yellow crocuses were peeping out of the soil, and Stella spotted a blue robin's egg. They were children now, and they were still holding hands.

"Wanna race?" Stella asked.

"Sure," Robert replied, knowing that even if she was a girl, those long legs of hers could burn up the turf in strides to match his own.

"Ready, set, go!" Stella cried, and the two ran along the meandering brook, their childish laughter filling the meadow with joyous sounds as they raced together toward eternity.

NURSING TIP #6: Warm up your stethoscope in your bare hands before placing it on your patient's bare chest.

****

Ellen's hair was quite naturally the color of wheat and she had a lovely ivory complexion and huge pale blue eyes. Some residents said that she looked like an angel.
Some of the nursing staff, however, said that she looked like a priss. It wasn't just her fine boned

features or even her small upturned nose. Ellen carried herself with an air of dignity that many mistook for a background of privilege.

If only they knew, Ellen thought wryly.

Ellen Jean Hooker had lived the first 17 years of her life in a way that would throw a dark shadow over all of the years that came afterward. Some have opined that those who choose the healing professions are attempting to heal something within themselves. Ellen wasn't sure about that but her childhood had certainly been mean.

Her father, when drunk, would beat Ellen's mother and torment her by threatening to kill the children that he insisted could not be his. Even so, Ellen thought as she held her sobbing little brother, that didn't seem like much of a reason to kill them.

Mark Hooker, Ellen's brother, was five years her junior. Although he would eventually stand a foot taller and outweigh her by over a hundred pounds, she would feel protective toward him for all of her life. "When I get big enough," he told Ellen, "I'm going to beat the crap out of him."

He never got the chance. Mark was 14 when they got the phone call. Daniel Hooker had been shot to death in a barroom brawl over a woman who was not their mother. By then, Ellen was living in Florida. It was Mark who called her. By the following Christmas, Mark was big enough to have carried out his threat.

****

Young Ellen Jean Hooker had but two goals. The first was to lose the hated surname of Hooker. The second was to get out of the tiny Texas truck stop that passed for a town.

When she accidentally got pregnant she inadvertently met both of those goals. Her mother cried and her father called her a tramp. Ellen didn't care. Her name was going to be Ellen Patrick and she and her husband were going to live in Galveston by the sea that she had always loved.

Jim Patrick was not, at age 18, ready to be a father. Ellen thought he should try. Melissa was a fussy, colicky baby who looked like a wizened old man.

Ellen and Jim were two perfectly nice people who managed to bring out the very worst in each other. They fought deep into the night while baby Melissa screamed and screamed. Soon the couple had no dishes because Ellen had smashed them all during one of their fights. Soon afterward, Jim punched holes in every wall of their apartment. Given that the walls were made of stucco that had to have been a painful experience for Jim.

At first, Ellen didn't mind so much. She had Melissa and her life was still better than it had been at home. But after a time she came to believe that there must be more to life than fighting and screaming. When she told Jim that she was taking Melissa and leaving, he shrugged.

Making Ends Meet was something that Ellen struggled with for years. She was often impatient with the daughter that she loved more than life itself. Fortunately, Melissa grew into a happy and easygoing child ...... traits that had come from Ellen knew not where.

For a few years after she left Jim, Ellen dated casually. After awhile, she didn't even do that. Working, raising Melissa and paying bills took up so much of her life that it was actually easy to shut down that part of herself. And she had almost forgotten that side of her soul existed until the day she changed shift with a nurse named Michael Iselin.

****

85

NURSING TIP #7: One of the most useful words in the English language is "Oh." When there are no words but something must be said, "Oh" can convey concern without criticism, empathy without pity, understanding without judgement.

****

"I don't care," Tasha was saying to Ellen. "I am not going back in that room."

"Why not?"

"Because she's hateful and if I go back in there I'll end up saying something I'll regret."

Ellen was puzzled. Mrs. Parker had seemed nice enough when she had given her the insulin shot. Thanked her, in face, and called her a lovely nurse. And Tasha seemed like a good aide. More like amazing if you considered her resident load.

"Is she confused?" Ellen asked.

"Oh no. Mrs. Parker's all there. She knows exactly what she's saying."

"OK. I'll talk to her," Ellen said.

"Why, hello dear,Mrs. Parker greeted her as she knocked on the door.

"Hello, ma'am. May I come in?"

"Come in, come in. Sit down, love, you look tired."

"Thank you, " Ellen replied, lowering herself into a worn armchair that Mrs. Parker had indicated.

"How are you?" Ellen asked.

"Fine, fine. Except I don't like that girl."

"Tasha?"

"Whatever her name is. The one that came in to make my bed."

"What's the problem?"

"The problem? Well, dear, isn't it obvious? She's a nigger."

Ellen felt the color drain from her face. "I'm sorry," she said. "I didn't hear you."

"A nigger. I said she's a nigger! And I don't want her black hands touching my things."

Now Ellen heard a humming in her head. "Oh," she replied. "Well it hurts me to hear you say that. You see, Tasha and I are sisters."

"No! You and her? Really?"

"Really and truly. You see, we had different fathers. Of course, we have no idea who our fathers were, mind you. You see, our mother was a .... well, you understand. She was a working woman. Worked mostly nights."

"Oh my."

"Yes and she had so many kids that me and Tasha .... well, you understand. We had to work nights too, when we got old enough."

"Oh dear!"

"Well, we all do what we have to do to survive. Oh yeah, do you want your pills."

"I wouldn't take anything from you, you, you, you whore! Send the other nurse in."

"Oh, you mean Michael? The man?"

"A man nurse! What, I get a choice between a whore and a queer? I'm going to report this."

"Now, Michael's not queer, just because he lives with that black man he says is his brother. He could be his brother. Look at Tasha and me. Besides, I doubt he's queer because he sure knows how to kiss a woman's ...."

"Get out of here, you bitch! Get out!"

"Yes, ma'am."

Back at her med cart, Ellen sighed. She knew she certainly hadn't handled that one according to anything she had ever learned in nursing school or anywhere else. And she really didn't care.

****

NURSING TIP #8: Petroleum jelly prevents a myriad of skin problems, from diaper rash to decubitus ulcers and it works better and costs less than almost anything else you might find. Just remember how slippery it is before putting it on your patient's feet.

****

Stella sighed. She was hungry this morning. Those two little silver dollar pancakes hadn't filled her up and she would be damned if she was going to eat that cement oatmeal they served. What was going on in the kitchen anyway? The food here used to be good.

Of course, she could ask Tasha to get her a bowl of Corn Flakes and a banana, but the poor girl looked harassed lately, ever since the other two aides had been let go.

"We're working short, Miss Vaughn," Tasha told her earlier. "I'm not supposed to tell you that, but it's the truth. And since I know you can mostly manage, I'll be back to help you with your hair about 11:00. I'm sorry, Miss Vaughn."

11:00! Why it would be lunch time before she could go to the main resident area!

"That's OK, baby," she replied. "I don't feel like going anywhere this morning anyhow."

****

NURSING TIP#9: Never tolerate incompetence in your aides and stand up for them against those who treat them disrespectfully. They are not just there to assist you. The entire efficiency of your unit depends largely upon their skill.

****

Unlike most nurses, Ellen never minded "floating", or being sent to a unit that was not her normally scheduled wing. Most nurse complained that they were at a disadvantage working unfamiliar territory, but Ellen always figured that the unexpected could happen anywhere.

"Stella Vaughn?"

"Yes, what's left of her," the old woman replied.

"Hi. I'm Ellen, your nurse today."

"Well come on in. Don't be shy."

Ellen entered the room, medicine cup and water cup in hand.

"I have your medicine, Mrs. Vaughn," the nurse said.

"Call me 'Stella', please," she replied, studying the nurse's face. My, Stella thought, but she was a pretty one.

"Are you married, dear?" she asked the pretty nurse.

"No ma'am. Not anymore."

Stella nodded, knowing all too well the pain of broken marriages to ask any more questions.

"Don't call me 'ma'am'", she said instead. "It makes me feel like an old lady."

Ellen grinned. Stella took her medicine and handed the empty cups back to Ellen.

There was a knock on the door. It was Michael, the nice young man who was a nurse. Stella thought that nursing was an odd field for a young fellow but she didn't care. Michael had given her better care than some of the silly female chits they'd had in there lately.

"Hi Stella," he said. And to the nurse, "Hey Ellen, got any Extra Strength Tylenol? There's none in the med room and Central Supply says acetaminophen, any strength, is no longer a stock item."

Ellen stared at Michael, her eyes widening. Acetaminophen no longer a stock item? Yesterday, it had been multiple vitamins with iron and last week it had been triple antibiotic ointment. Was the new management insane?

"Yes, I can spare some," she replied. "I'll bring it down to your hall in a moment."

"Thanks," he replied.

After he left, Stella asked, "Is he your boyfriend?"

"H-How ...." Ellen stammered, a furious blush rising in her ivory complexion.

Stella smiled gently. "I don't know how dear. I just know. They say your eyes get worse as you get older, but in some ways they get better. You see more subtle things. You can pick up on more nuances. Maybe it's just because you have more time on your hands to figure things out."

Ellen mumbled a goodbye and returned to her medicine cart. If what Stella said was true, Ellen thought, then she'd better watch her nuances around here. It would not in any way benefit her to have made common knowledge that she and Michael had become involved.

It had begun innocently enough, Ellen thought, feeling even then as if she were pleading her case before an unsympathetic jury. Sure, she'd been attracted to Michael Iselin from the moment she first saw him but it wasn't until the night the hurricane winds tore the roof off of the North Wing that she had ended up in his arms.

It was at the end of a 36-hour shift for both of them. Ellen was tired and shaken. She was also exhausted from conveying to her residents and staff that everything was under control and that the roof blowing off the wing was absolutely no reason at all to panic. At first, Michael had hugged her like a friend would. At first.

That had been in September. September in Florida usually means the beginning of the end of the daily torrential downpours and the most violent lightning on Earth. Ellen never did figure out exactly why Florida is called "The Sunshine State."

September is also the zenith of hurricane season. Swirling patterns spun out from the Caribbean Sea nightly on the Weather Channel. No one paid much attention when the tropical wave from Africa was upgraded to Tropical Storm Linda.

They did, however, pay attention when it started to look like Hurricane Linda was headed their way.

"Ever been through a hurricane?" asked Susan, who was working North Wing with her. That had been a good day. North Wing had two nurses working the floor.

"Yes," Ellen answered. "But not here."

"Well, I am telling you right now, there isn't anything at all like a Florida hurricane. If this baby hits, you'd better be prepared."

And Ellen did not reply at that, at least with a hurricane, you could be prepared. Ellen was from Texas and had long ago learned the terrible power of wind.

In the days that followed, the staff at the Florida Forest busied themselves with stocking the wing closets with bottle water, flashlights and batteries while the skeletal maintenance staff crew purchased plywood. There didn't seem to be as much bottled water this year and there were rumors that matches, cheaper than flashlights, were going to be used. In the past, the use of candles following a hurricane had been prohibited as a safety hazard.

By the end of the week, it was clear that the Florida Forest stood directly in what appeared to be Hurricane Linda's probable path. The outgoing shift was asked to stay. The incoming shift was called in early. Noncritical patients from the regional hospital were transferred to the Florida Forest. Plywood was nailed across windows.

It was considered too dangerous to the wandering residents to fill up any bathtubs or whirlpools, although sinks in locked areas like med rooms were filled to capacity. The residents were brought, beds and all, into hallways and interior windowless rooms.

And then the Florida Forest waited.

****

Stella knew the storm was near when everything got unearthly quiet. There was no sound anywhere. No rustle of a leaf, no cricket, no bird.

And then the wind began to blow.

"You're not afraid, are you Miss Vaughn?" Tasha asked.

"Heavens no, dear," Stella replied.

****

The advantage of a hurricane over a tornado is that with a hurricane, the wind blows in only one direction at a time.

There is probably no advantage to a tornado but if there were one, it would be that a tornado does not continue for hours on end.

Ellen had already had her first heart-stopping moment of the shift, when a head count failed to account for Mrs. Sunderland, North Wing's most notorious wanderer. Tasha found her huddled in a corner in the shower.

"Which isn't a bad place to be during a hurricane," Michael had remarked. "I mean, they say she's crazy, but she has more sense than you do, Nurse, standing there in front of the window."

Ellen had been standing in front of the window. There hadn't been enough plywood to go around, and Ellen had been peering through an

96

uncovered window, straining her eyes for a sign of the tiny, elderly woman in the storm.

"I was looking for Mrs. Sunderland," she answered.

"I know," he said. "But really, Ellen, take care of yourself first. If you get hurt who's going take care of your patients.?"

And Ellen was thinking that she had never noticed before just how deep his dark eyes were.

No, she wasn't just now noticing. She was acknowledging what she had been noticing for some time.

The winds began to scream so furiously that they had to shout.

"Hold the flashlight, Michael. I can't even see how much insulin I'm drawing up in this syringe. Is it day or night?"

"Who knows? Who cares?"

"I care. I'm passing meds."

"Ellen, Ellen," he shouted. "Look at the advantage of working during a hurricane."

"And what might that be?" she hollered back.

"No chance of a lightning strike." he yelled.

And Ellen laughed as if he had just said the funniest thing she had ever heard. She was thinking that she was either falling head over heels in love with Michael or she was getting punch drunk from lack of sleep. And she had no way of knowing that Michael was thinking that her laughter sounded just like bells.

And that was when the roof was torn off the North Wing of the Florida Forest.

Michael and Ellen had been preparing meds. Susan had been flushing a G-tube run by auxillary power. Mary had been comforting a frightened resident. Tasha and Rose had been trying to convince Mrs. Sunderland that now was not a good time to go out into the courtyard. Robert Bishop had actually been sleeping.

No one who had been on North Wing that day would ever forget the sound of the roof being removed or the sight of the open sky above them, although most of them would certainly try.

Afterward, there was near bedlam trying to get the residents located to other wings that were still intact. Miraculously, no one was hurt, not even when the glass from an uncovered window flew about the wing in jagged pieces.

And afterward, somehow, Ellen ended up at Michael's house, which was a good 20 miles from the Florida Forest.

"It looks like the hurricane didn't even hit here," Ellen remarked.

"Nah. Just rearranged a few mailboxes.

Ellen smiled and they fell silent, each of them thinking about what they had seen during the seemingly endless drive back to Michael's house.

Smashed housing developments with trees on top of roofs. Trailer parks with a million little pieces of metal and plywood. Roads blocked by the twisted, tangled roots of trees that had stood for 300 years. And water, absolutely everywhere.

Here and there, they would spot a teddy bear or a photograph. There was no way of knowing to whom these items belonged or how far the winds had carried them.

Ellen and Michael were beyond exhaustion. They had pushed themselves for 36 hours without rest. They had been in mortal danger. They had seen destruction. And their tired brains would not stop forming the memories that would make them uneasy with the sound of wind for months to come.

"Michael?"

"Ellen?"

And then it happened. She was in his arms, he was in her arms and suddenly, they were a tangle of of arms.

I can't believe it, Michael thought. It's really happening. Here he was, he was actually kissing Ellen's soft pink mouth, something he had been thinking about for months. But no. Shit! She was pulling away from him.

"Michael, no. We can't. It would be wrong."

"Ellen, if it's because we work together I'll quit this minute."

"No, she answered." "It's not that."

"Then what?" he asked gently. "Why would it be wrong?"

"Because we've been wearing these clothes for two days now."

Michael threw back his curly, dark head of hair and laughed out loud.

Oh God, Ellen thought. I't happening and it's not just because we're both half loony from lack of sleep. It's really happening.

"OK," Michael said. "Good point. We'll take a shower first."

"Together," Ellen answered.

"Together," he agreed.

They stood in the alcove of the shower then and a moment of awkwardness passed between them, as is not uncommon in people right before they see each other naked for the first time.

"Would you like an undressing room?" Michael asked, indicating a small room to the left of what Ellen thought must be the bedroom. "I think there's a robe hanging on the inside of the door."

Ellen shook her head. There was no need to be shy. She had a good body and she knew it.

Michael's pupils, almost invisible in his dark eyes, were growing wider. Damn. He had never realized just how much a nursing uniform hid.

"What?" she asked, the faintest trace of a rosy blush spreading across her creamy ivory skin.

"You're beautiful, Ellen. You're absolutely beautiful."

And Ellen wished that there was a word that she could use. Michael was too robustly masculine to call handsome.

But her pupils were widening too.

Too bad you can't really call a man beautiful in our culture, Ellen thought as she rubbed soapy lather over his broad shoulders, his wide chest, his narrow waist, his compact buttocks and his strong thighs. Because Michael was beautiful and the sight of his rugged beauty, his intoxicating maleness, was awaking in Ellen deep emotions she had not felt in nearly a decade.

God, she's even more beautiful than I had imagined, Michael thought as she rinsed pink, purple and blue soap bubbles from her lovely curves. She was slender yet she was voluptuous.

And afterward, they walked to the bedroom holding hands. But the bed was so soft and warm and comfortable and they were so tired.

"Michael?"

"Hmmmmmmmmmmmmmmmmm."

And they fell asleep then, her long blonde hair trailing across the dark hairs of his chest, both of them looking more like children exhausted after a hard day of play than two adults who had been about to make love.

****

The human vertebral column is comprised of 26 bones, starting with the atlas high up in the neck and terminating with the coccyx, which is really three to five individual bones fused into one. It was there, in those three to five fused bones, that Ellen felt a definite pressure that woke her up.

For a moment she was lost, and then it all came back to her. The hurricane, the drive home, Michael.

Michael's deep even breathing told her that he was still asleep. And suddenly, Ellen knew what was causing the pressure on her tailbone.

A giggle escaped her throat before she could contain it. It had been so long since she had slept in the same bed as a man that she had forgotten.

A man's penis wakes up long before he does.

Turning, she took in the sight of the still slumbering Michael. The sunlight fell in slants across his face and chest.

He is so beautiful, she thought as she traced her fingers across his body.

Michael opened his eyes and smiled sleepily at Ellen.

"Good morning," he murmured.

They were both still naked.

There was no awkwardness between them this time as they embraced. It is hard to say which one of them started it but soon they were kissing deeply. And Ellen could feel that tingling that signals the increased blood flow of arousal.

It had been so long.

And then he was holding her breasts in his warm hands and kissing them and she could feel herself growing wetter each time his lips brushed across her nipples.

Hungrily, she responded by covering his chest and abdomen with kisses of her own.

"Stop, stop," Michael said, holding her at arm's length. "I want to look at you."

She could feel his eyes brush across her breasts and pelvis and her body responded as if he were touching her.

"Oh Michael," she whispered. "I want you."

They embraced again, holding each other tighter and closer, trying to get as close as one human possibly can to another.

Michael's mouth was hard on hers, his kiss demanding and possessive.

It was mid-morning and sunlight was streaming brilliantly into the room despite the drawn curtains. Sometimes, Ellen was aware of the golden light around her, the cruelly beautiful sunshine that follows a hurricane.

But then another sensation would pass over her and it would not be day at all, or even night.

Her legs parted and Michael pulled her hips even closer to his. And they tried, as humans always have, to merge into one being.

Oh God, he was entering her now and the feeling was so exquisite that Ellen began to tremble. Michael responded with a touch that was sweetly gentle.

And then with one that was not.

And she responded, giving in to a passion that she had long since forgotten, as they both reached to join their hearts and souls and bodies into one entity until there was no sunshine or city in ruins or even Earth, only Michael and Ellen alone in a vast and endless universe.

****

Melissa Patrick hung up the telephone in exasperation.

"Missy, forget it," her father said, using his pet name for her. "You can't place any calls in or out of Florida right now. The circuits are a mess."

"But Dad, I have to know if Mom's alright."

"Your mother's alright," Jim Patrick answered with a confidence he did not feel, not after having seen the news of the storm on television.

"How do you know?"

"Because if she wasn't, someone would contact us."

"But how? You just said ...."

And Jim felt, not for the first time, the humbling that parents feel when they realize that their children have developed sophisticated capabilities and can no longer be comforted by simple answers.

"Okay, honey," he admitted. "I don't know. But since there's no way to communicate with her right now, I'd rather not have us go nuts wondering. I feel she's alright, OK? I feel it in my heart."

"OK," Melissa answered, old enough to understand that until communications were restored, that feeling was all they could rely on.

Melissa Patrick was 15 years old. She had the dubious blessing of her mother's beauty and her father's good looks. Like all progeny, she had traits from both of her parents within her as well as a few characteristics that were all her own.

One thing that was all her own was a sense of well-being. Melissa was an exceptionally content teenager. Due to the year-round school program in Florida, Melissa was able to spend a week in Texas with her father and his family every few months. Melissa liked the time in Galveston. Her stepmother, Patty, was almost like an older sister. And their son Brian was, of course, her brother.

The rest of the time Melissa lived in Florida with her mother.

Melissa liked having two lives, two families. She knew that none of her friends could understand her attitude but Melissa could not remember a time when her parents had lived together under the same roof.

In all of Melissa's memory, her father had been married to Patty.

And for all of Melissa's life, she'd had her mother all to herself.

****

NURSING TIP #10: There are organizations that bring dogs and other animals to visit the sick and the injured. Do everything you can to get them to come to your unit. With some types of hurt, animals have healing powers that humans simply do not possess.

****

PART THREE

Hurricane Linda had strained every available resource and service in the area, and it would be several months before the roof was replaced on the North Wing. But the reconstruction of North Wing would be complete before it no longer looked, at first glance, as if the hurricane was still going on.

The sabal palmettos and coconut palms were too flexible to have been ripped from the ground like so many citrus and cypress trees, but they remained bent, all in the same direction, a frozen tribute to the storm's power.

Mary thought it gave the Florida Forest a surreal look and she was tired of looking at it. Mary had lost her trailer to the storm. Now she and the kids were living with her mother and that was really getting on everyone's nerves.

Mary Drennan had been a single parent for so long that it barely seemed like a burden anymore. And lately things had been hopeful, with the kids getting older and the governor's new proposal that might free John by this spring.

And then a damned hurricane had to blow her home into a thousand pieces.

And it wasn't just that. Her job was becoming nearly impossible to perform. Yesterday, they'd had only two aides for 40 residents, and they'd waited nearly half the shift for the first linen delivery.

Many of the aides (The smart ones, Tasha would later say), had already quit, but Mary was not a quitter. She was a giver. And she kept right on giving, spreading herself thinner and working harder than ever before, ignoring the insidious weariness that accompanies overwork.

Because that, right or wrong, is the type of person that Mary Drennan was.

****

THE PRAYER OF STUDENT NURSES: Dear God, don't let me screw up and kill somebody today.

****

"Melissa, you open up this door!"

Melissa Patrick responded by cranking up something called Nine Inch Nails even louder on the stereo.

"Melissa!"

Ellen had just told her daughter about Michael Iselin and the girl was not taking the news well.

"Melissa!"

"What?"

"Open up this door or I'll ...."

There was a moment in which both Melissa and Ellen wondered what Ellen would say next.

"Or I'll bust the door down!" she finally shouted.

Melissa couldn't help but smile. Her mother was a small, delicately built woman. At 15 years old, Melissa was two inches taller and ten pounds heavier.

"Melissa!"

Then again, on Take Your Daughters To Work Day last year, Melissa had seen her small, delicately built mother lift patients twice her size. She opened up the door.

"And turn that stereo off," Ellen said, her eyes flashing in a way that made Melissa decide to turn the stereo off and not just lower the volume as she usually did when her mother told her to turn it off.

Mother and daughter faced each other now, eyes, eyes snapping and chests heaving. They loved each other more than anything else and were positively furious with each other.

"I'm sorry you're upset with me," Ellen began, "but you've got to understand that mothers are human too."

"Then at least find a real man!"

The urge to slap Melissa rose up high and ugly in Ellen. She fought the urge. She kicked it, slapped it, beat it down and stomped on it. Finally she managed to say, calmly even, "What do you mean by that?"

"C'mon, Mom. I've heard you say that a lot of the male nurses you know are gay."

"Not all of them. I never said all of them .... Melissa, he is not gay!"

"Maybe not. But even so, don't you find male nurses a little weird?"

"I do not. Do you find female doctors weird?"

112

"No, but you yourself said that a nursing home is primarily a woman's world. The nurses are women, the aides are women, even most of the patients are women. Young women taking care of old women. You once said ...."

"I once said too many things," Ellen snapped. "Melissa, Missy .... for God's sake! I will not apologize because he's not a lumberjack! Besides, that's not what's really bugging you and you know it! For the first time in your life I have a boyfriend. Melissa, honey, we need to talk about this."

"We can talk about whatever you want, Mom. But I'm not the only one who's going to give you grief about this. What about your bosses at work, Mom? Don't you think they'll try to hold this over your head? What about the other nurses? And the aides, what do you think they are going to say if they know that two of their bosses are sleeping together?"

Ellen stared at Melissa, wondering when she had grown up.

****

Melissa cranked up Nine Inch Nails again. Mom was right. Michael's being a nurse wasn't what was really bugging her.

It was Michael's being a man.

"What do you want?" Mom had asked her earlier. "Do you want me to just sit around and devote my entire life to you and only you?"

Yes, Mother, Melissa thought. I guess that is what I want.

It was what she'd always had and there had been no warming that it was going to stop. No warning at all.

Melissa didn't want to share her mother, least of all with someone she couldn't even brag about. Oh yes, Melissa, and what does your stepfather do for a living?

Damn you, Mother, Melissa thought.

And yet, Melissa had inherited Ellen's generous heart as well as her striking beauty. Somewhere deep, deep inside her teenage soul, Melissa truly wanted her mother to be happy.

"Melissa! Turn that stereo down, or I will bust it!"

Parents are so stupid, Melissa thought as she turned the volume down. Her mother had paid a lot of money for that stereo.

****

THE EVERYDAY PRAYER OF NURSES: Dear Lord, use me as an instrument of Your mercy, today and every day. Let my mind be sharp, my hands be skilled and my heart be gentle. Amen.

****

Marguerite Cannon was what the nurses called a "High Heels" as in "Here comes a High Heels". High Heels were nurses who no longer practiced nursing. Through education, seniority, longevity and back injury, these former floor nurses had been promoted to administrative posts. Florida Forest's new management had fired all of the existing High Heels and replaced them with their own.

High heeled shoes are, of course, prohibited in any clinical nursing position. The clickety-clack of Marguerite's heels on the tile floor of Ellen's unit alerted Ellen that she was probably in trouble.

"Your unit is not in order," Marguerite told Ellen. "You have call lights on, a shower chair in

115

the hallway and dirty linen on the floor in 212. You need to start writing your aides up."

Ellen's unit was most certainly not in order and she could only wonder at Marguerite's logic in being concerned about a towel on the floor when they were so understaffed.

"I have exactly two aides, again, and I'm the only nurse here. We are dangerously understaffed and I will not write the aides up for that!"

That was what Ellen said alright, but Marguerite Cannon walked away as soon as she finished speaking and she never heard Ellen's reply.

****

Sometimes in life, Mary had noticed, when one thing goes wrong it seems to set off a chain reaction. First her trailer was destroyed. Next her son Jason was arrested for possession of marijuana. After that she had to put Candy, her beloved spaniel, to sleep.

But the worst came when she got the news that John was not going to be given early release from prison after all.

"I'm sorry," Sgt. Tibbons said. "I thought maybe he would be included in the Governor's plan to cut down on prison overcrowding since he's really been a model inmate, but it's not possible. The proposal includes only nonviolent offenders.

John wasn't a violent offender, Mary thought. He was a father. A swimming instructor at the YMCA had molested their young daughter. John and Mary had filed charges but the instructor had been let off on a technicality and John had gone after the man.

Mary's greatest regret was that she hadn't gone after the bastard herself.

****

The nurses were getting downright ugly by the time the new administration agreed to a face-to-face meeting with the staff.

To their utter amazement, they were written up for the very concerns they voiced to management.

Michael spoke up first. The trays were always late, he said, because of the reduced kitchen staff and when the trays got there, there weren't enough aides to feed the residents while the food was still hot. Michael was written up because records revealed a greater than normal incidence of weight loss on his unit.

Susan spoke next, pointing out that routine care was nearly impossible without regular delivery of fresh linen. Susan was written up because several visitors had complained about residents, namely Susan's, looking unkempt.

"There is no excuse for this," Marguerite Cannon hissed. "The State can cite us, fine us, shut us down."

"Then do something to help us! Ellen cried. "How are we supposed to function with half the staff and a quarter of the supplies?"

"You know what your problem is?" Marguerite asked. "You're spoiled. The Church was overstaffed and overspent and that's why they had to sell. It's the 90's. Deal with it! Learn to do more with less. And if your aides are too lazy to take care of residents then fire them."

Ellen stared at Marguerite. "Look," she answered. "I've got about the best aides love, or money will buy, but they are not superhuman."

Marguerite snorted. "If they're so wonderful why does your unit always look so shabby?" And one of your wonderful aides, Mary Drennan I believe, isn't her husband in jail? For assault, isn't that right? Are you so sure she's the best person to be caring for your residents? After all, it's your license on the line."

Ellen was standing next to Susan but it was Michael, from across the room, who sensed something dangerous in Ellen. The nostrils of her finely boned upturned nose were flaring and her blue eyes were on fire.

Mary has been here 20 years, Ellen was thinking, and this bitch has been here less than two months and the place has gone to hell.

"Yes, my license is on the line," Ellen agreed, astonished that she could speak so clearly when she was barely breathing. "But it's you who place it there. You and everyone else who thinks that cutting essential staff and supplies is the best way to save a buck. The residents be damned as long as it looks good to the stockholders! And as far as my aides, I make no apologies for any of them. I doubt that I could do what they manage to do in a day.

"Oh?" Marguerite answered. "Well then, maybe the problem is you if you doubt you could do the work of your aides. Perhaps you aren't qualified to be in charge of a unit. You're a fairly new and inexperienced nurse, aren't you?"

"Oh for crying out loud!" Susan objected. "That's it! I'm out of here. I was at Rose Forest when you people took over. You screw up a place beyond repair and then try to blame the nurses. I honestly believe that after a couple of weeks here, Mother Teresa would start to look bad! You'll have my notice by the end of this shift."

"Don't bother," Marguerite replied. "You can leave now."

****

THE PRAYER OF NURSES PRESENT AT THE DEATHBED: Heavenly Father, Help me to be not afraid but instead to be strong so that I might help others, both those who have gone to You and those, grief stricken, left behind. Amen.

****

Robert Bishop reached for the packet hidden deep inside his eyeglass case, where no one would think to look. The folded up paper pill cup was no longer white and it looked as withered and worn as the hand that held it.

Robert took a deep breath. The battered paper held his heart medicine for the past three weeks, pills that the nurses had charted as given

120

because they didn't know he had hidden the pills in his cheek instead of swallowing them.

Opening the packet, he counted 20 pills. More than enough and then some. The tiny yellow tablets were none other than digitalis, derived from the common foxglove plant and deadly in all but the smallest of concentrations.

Looking out the window, he noted the full moon. This would be a good night to carry out his plan. The full moon always caused some of the residents to go wild and the staff would have their hands full tonight. No one would notice him.

The only thought bothering Robert Henry Bishop at that moment was the nagging fear that God would not forgive him for taking his own life.

But surely God would understand. Wasn't He all wise and all knowing? For if He were, then surely He would see that Robert wasn't really committing suicide. He was dying and he wanted to die while he still had some dignity left.

Robert had no other particular worries or concerns on this night. His children and grandchildren would be sad but they would accept his death as natural and inevitable. After all, he was a very old man.

The only other person who crossed his mind was Stella. He didn't want to leave her but he couldn't let her see the scarecrow shell of a man he would soon become.

"Stella," he whispered to the full moon. "If I stick around much longer I'm going to be so sick and in so much pain that I'll probably say hateful things to you that I don't mean. If I leave now, you can remember for the rest of your life that I loved you."

There was no one else that Robert could think of. It was funny to be so old and so alone with so few people who would be affected by his death.

Robert took one last look around the room. The moonlight fell across the sleeping form of Mr. Ellis, his roommate. Mr. Ellis was in the final stages of Alzheimer's disease. He stared listlessly into space all day, never uttering a sound. Once, about a year ago, Robert had seen him smile.

"See you shortly, fellow," Robert whispered.

He heard a high pitched scream in the hallway. The sound did not alarm him. It was only Mrs. Jacobs. She would scream and curse for the next half hour or so and accuse the nurses of stealing her mother's china and linen. Finally, and only after she had managed to slap one of the aides, would she cry herself to sleep.

And during her crying jag, Robert knew, one of the aides would cover her with a blanket and fluff up her pillow, murmuring a few comforting words. More often than not it would be the same aide she had smacked earlier.

Robert had to wonder at the staff. Certainly, he would not put up with what they did, not for any amount of money. But he supposed that someone had to. After all, but for the grace of God, he would be as fruity as Mrs. Jacobs.

And it seemed as if His grace was running out. Which is what brought him to this moment, why he was about to swallow 20 digitalis tablets.

He could swallow them down with the water that Ellen had brought him earlier and lay down on his back, the way he always slept. That way, when the staff found him ....

The staff.

A new and troubling thought occurred to Robert. The staff could be held accountable for what he was about to do. If anything went wrong and there was an investigation or an autopsy ....

123

In the past few weeks Robert had come to depend upon the nurses in a way he never had before. He needed pain medication now.

Robert remembered hearing Ellen at the change of shift one evening, right after Dr. Johnson had given him the news.

"He's been diagnosed as terminal and he has a PRN order for Roxanol. He's not the type of complain so please, make sure he's not in pain."

And Michael, the night nurse, had done just that. As busy as they were, these nurses seemed to come around with the medicine before the pain became excruciating.

And the nurses were busy these days. After the Church had sold the place it seemed there were less staff. Furthermore, Robert figured the State must be mad at the place about something, for their investigators kept popping up unannounced and asking questions in a way that made it seem as if the nurses and aides were doing something wrong. Of course, given the staff shortage, they couldn't be doing everything right.

Robert thought of Ellen and Michael and the others and imagined them undergoing a State investigation into just how Mr. Bishop had managed to receive 20 times the prescribed dosage of digitalis.

And Robert knew he could not go through with it.

One by one, he dropped the pills into the air conditioning unit and then laid down on the bed. He fell asleep to the hallway sounds of a full moon.

It must have been after midnight when the pain awoke him, Robert decided, for it was too quiet to still be evening. He could hear Mr. Ellis' even breathing. Jesus, his hip hurt!

Robert put the call light on. Christ, to be begging for morphine in the middle of the night like this!

The door opened and Robert was puzzled at the flash of golden hair. He thought that Ellen had left hours ago. But no, it wasn't Ellen. Why, she wasn't even a nurse, not with that long green dress. The dress looked so familiar to Robert, yet he could not place where he had seen it before.

The woman moved across the room to his bed and he remembered where he had seen the dress at the same moment he looked with astonished disbelief at the most perfect face he had ever known.

Fifty years of marriage, three children, eight grandchildren and the past 20 years without her had never happened. Marion Susan Walker stood before him looking exactly as she had the first time he had ever seen her, at that long ago church picnic, wearing a dress that exactly matched the color of her eyes.

"Marion," he breathed.

She put a finger to her lips, green eyes sparkling. She held out her slender hand and he took it, rising easily out of the bed. The pain had completely vanished. To his astonishment, Mr. Ellis waved at them and winked.

They went out into the hall and Robert saw Roger and Dave, the fellows from the funeral home. They were carrying a stretcher. It must be morning after all, for there was Ellen closing all of the room doors up and down the hall, the way they always did whenever Roger and Dave had to carry and ex-resident out of the building. To his amazement, he hear Ellen give Roger his name and room number.

Still holding Marion's hand, he walked with her toward the exit. No one seemed to notice them.

Robert looked at Tasha. Tasha was sad but she was also relieved. Tasha now had too many residents to care for and Mr. Bishop's death meant maybe, just maybe, her remaining residents could get better care today. Robert could look right into her soul and see that.

Ellen looked tired and that line Robert had noticed lately was forming between her eyes. She had liked Mr. Bishop and would miss him. She hoped he had not suffered in his last hours. She was also concerned that the protocol and paperwork required for a Discharge by Death Report (due within the hour of expiration) would mean that, once again, her residents would have to wait for their medication and treatments. Robert could look right into Ellen's soul and see that too.

As he and Marion left the wing, he heard Michael say, "It's OK, Ellen. He slept peacefully all night, never woke up or put the call light on even once."

****

THE PRAYER OF NURSES WHO WITNESS UNTIMELY DEATH: Father in Heaven, help me to abate my anger, for in it is self-righteousness. Lord, help me to remember that I am not You.

****

The human body contains a number of fluids that, while they do very well on the inside of the body, are disastrous if they by some chance end up on the outside. The most notable example of this is hydrochloric acid, a normal component of stomach juice. Hydrochloric acid's extremely low pH inhibits all but a very few bacteria from multiplying and probably explains why we don't become deathly ill every time we eat. However, hydrochloric acid was never meant to come in contact with our skin.

Miss Lilly had pulled out her own gastric tube, fully inflated 30cc balloon and all. As anyone who works with the confused can tell you, this is not an unusual occurence. Residents have been known to pull out gastric tubes, IV lines, even urinary catheters. The problem was, no one noticed for several hours and the stomach juices had plenty of time to seep out of the stoma and onto Lilly's skin. By the time Mary saw it, Miss Lilly had caustic burns on her abdomen.

Marguerite Cannon blamed Ellen. Ellen blamed the new administration. Mary blamed herself.

"It's not your fault," Rose told her. "You can't be everywhere at once."

But Mary had checked up on Lilly. She just hadn't checked under Lilly's blanket.

For Mary, it was a moment of truth. Her workload was double what it once had been. In order to get her work done she was taking dangerous shortcuts and her resident had gotten hurt as a result.

"I can't take this anymore," she told Ellen. "We are working so short that no one is safe in this place. I'm giving my notice. I've got to either find another job or another line of work."

And Ellen knew better than to try to talk Mary out of leaving.

Naturally, the hospital that Miss Lilly was sent to reported the obvious neglect.

"There will be hell to pay," Marguerite fairly yelled at Ellen. "They could shut this place down."

And Ellen, who had been working 16 days straight without a day off, hardly recognized her own voice as she answered, "Good. Because God knows, someone should."

****

THE PRAYER OF NURSES WHO WORK SHORT STAFFED: Dear Lord, Do not let me give in to stressful anxiety. Don't let me forget that a warm smile or a gentle touch may be the best medicine I can give today. Amen.

****

"Miss Vaughn, you OK in there?" Tasha called through the closed door.

"Yes dear, I'm fine. Just a little slow this morning."

Stella was sitting on the toilet, waiting and and waiting for what she doubted would come. If anyone were to ask her what was the worst part about growing old she would have to say it was what happened to your bowels. Stella knew not to strain. Dr. Patel had warned her that straining on the toilet could put undue pressure on her heart.

"Miss Vaughn, you want me to lay out your clothes while you're in there?" Tasha called.

"I wish you would call me 'Stella'," she called back.

"I know, but I keep forgetting. It's just the way I was brought up. Older people should be treated with respect. Why, in China a woman of your aged would be highly revered."

"Well, I wonder if in China a woman of my age could move her bowels."

"Want me to bring you some warm prune juice, Miss Vaughn?"

"Honey, I've tried prune juice, fiber, Milk of Magnesia and every suppository ever manufactured. I think I'm just too old to shit."

"When did you last go?"

"Oh, I don't know. A week or so, I guess."

"A week or so! Why didn't you tell me?"

"I'm telling you now."

"No, I mean why didn't you tell me earlier?:

And Stella responded with the most exasperating words a nurse or nurse's aide will ever hear:

"Well dear, I didn't want to be a bother."

****

THE PRAYER OF NURSES WHO WORK DANGEROUSLY SHORT STAFFED: Father in Heaven, be with me.

****

Stella really didn't want to be a bother. She knew the staff was under tremendous fire. She could see it in Tasha's harried face and in the dark circles under Ellen's eyes. She'd heard it in the tightly controlled impatience in Susan's voice before she, too, had quit.

Besides, Stella didn't mind sitting on the toilet all that much. It was as warm and comfortable there as anywhere else and it gave her a chance to think.

Robert Bishop had passed away the other night. Stella wondered where he was now. Well, she could be sure he wasn't sitting on a toilet trying to get his old body to perform functions he had once taken for granted.

Rose, the night aide, had come to her last night. Rose knew that Stella had spent much time in Robert's company and she was concerned about Stella.

In all of her life, Stella had rarely been without a man. She'd had five husbands and numerous lovers and she had loved them all.

Or thought that she had, until she met John Vaughn.

In her one hundredth year of life Stella found true love. She and John married shortly thereafter. And the brevity of their time together mattered not one iota, for their hearts had known each other for all of their lives.

Though it had taken one hundred years, Stella felt blessed to have found that love at all.

And if there was Life after Death, then Stella knew that John Vaughn would be waiting for her on the other side.

Oh, but she would miss Robert Bishop. How she would miss him.

No point in bawling, Stella told herself sternly. At 104, you're old enough to know that there's some things in life you can't do a damned thing about.

And so, instead of crying, Stella peed instead, silently thanking God that her kidneys, at least, were still working.

****

THE PRAYER OF NURSES WHO WORK CRIMINALLY SHORT STAFFED: Father in Heaven, forgive me for those I did not help. My mind and bones are weary and I can do no more than I did today. Father forgive me. Amen.

****

The first lunch trays were on the floor before Ellen ever got to Stella's room.

"Stella, I called your doctor and I have something to help you move your bowels."

"What, a stick of dynamite?"

Ellen smiled and handed her a glass of what looked and tasted like vegetable oil. Then she went over to Glenda's bed and shut off the gastric feeding pump so she could medicate her and flush the tube.

They had been so short staffed lately that sometimes at night no one ever came in to check on them unless Stella put the call light on. Stella had taken to watching over her speechless roommate.

"Honey, I wonder if you could check that thing on her left heel."

And even before Ellen looked, she had a sinking feeling of what she would find.

With all of the staff cuts, there was no way the aides were turning every immobile resident every two hours any more than the nurses were administering every ordered medication or treatment.

What Ellen saw was a centimeter wide, second stage decubitus ulcer. The angry red tissue told her that there was still blood circulation to the area and that with treatment, Glenda's foot would heal.

"I figured you'd know what it was," Stella was saying. "And that you'd know what to do."

Ellen knew what it was. She didn't want to tell Stella that it was a well developed bedsore and that a resident, not the staff, had finally noticed it.

****

PART FOUR

Things got worse at the Florida Forest before they got better.

Tasha very nearly quit one day in March when she went a double shift without having any fresh linen at all. There was no one working in the laundry that day.

Marguerite Cannon, breath minty from the antacid tablets she now chewed continuously, pleaded with her to stay.

A week earlier, she'd been pleading with Rose.

Rose Cummings had begun her career at the Florida Forest in 1972, a full decade and a half before Congress insisted that nurse's aides in all states be certified. Rose could remember when practices such as double diapering and arbitrary use of restraints had been allowed. Before the Sunshine Unit was built in 1978, confused residents had been locked up on the East Wing, with little or no opportunity to ever see the outdoors.

Marguerite Cannon tried to get Rose to stay, but Rose was beyond anything Marguerite or anyone else could say. The final straw for Rose was when Carmen, one of the residents Rose had gotten after Mary left, weighed in at 69 pounds, which represented at least a 10 pound weight loss from her normal baseline. Carmen's daughter had screamed at Rose. Rose knew that Carmen's weight was down because no one had time to supervise her and stop her from tossing her food into the azalea bushes at mealtime.

Rose Cummings had spent the past 25 years of her life caring for the residents behind the gracious, rose covered brick wall of the Florida Forest, and she had never seen anything like the things she'd seen in the past year.

****

Tasha ended up staying, although her reasons had nothing to do with anything anyone else had said to her.

Tasha Phillips was only 22 years old, but she had an enormous faith in herself and her work. Tasha knew that her leaving would not change things, it would only remove her from the situation. And she believed that the situation could be worse if someone else were to take her place. Certainly, she didn't see how anyone else could do any better than she had done.

In the end, Tasha stayed because she believed that someone had to stay.

****

Marguerite Cannon was growing desperate. This job was supposed to cinch her career and she had followed every rule to ensure that the facility made a large profit under her administration. But the rules had not allowed for the vulnerability of frail residents who could not be budgeted like so many pens and paper clips.

Marguerite had gone to nursing school in the early 1960's, when nursing students were still instructed to rise and relinquish their seats whenever a physician entered the nurses' station. She had been only 20 years old.

Few young nurses were as idealistic and altruistic as Marguerite had been in her early days. She truly believed that love and faith could conquer all and the field of nursing seemed to suit her beliefs.

Unfortunately, Marguerite was never able to reconcile the wide discrepancy between nursing theory and nursing practice. The Boston hospital where she was employed at was understaffed at best. Pain-racked patients screamed at her because she couldn't get their medicine to them fast enough. Family members screamed at her because they couldn't or wouldn't scream at the doctor. Harried doctors, out of time and out of patience, screamed at her. Marguerite had not expected the gentle art of nursing to involve so much screaming.

Despite this, she became a good nurse. A good nurse who hated her job. When she was offered a promotion that would get her off the unit floor, she jumped.

Marguerite spent the next five years learning how to be a leader, a teacher and an administrator. Then she quit her job because she and Bob had decided to raise a family.

It would be fifteen years before Marguerite would again enter the workplace, years in which she had done more than raise her family. Marguerite had by then earned her MBA as well as her MSN.

At first, it had been terrifying. So much had changed! Computers, women in leadership positions .... Marguerite nearly fled back home to her family that first day on the job. But she was a quick study. She always had been. And last year, when she'd been offered this position, she knew it would be the last job of her career. If she could pull this off, if the Florida Forest could net a fat profit under her administration, she and Bob could retire early and enjoy life a little before it was too late.

Instead, Marguerite mused, she'd be lucky if she didn't end up going to jail.

Corporate was screaming at her. The investors were screaming at her. Her staff was screaming at her.

Nursing, for Marguerite, had come full circle.

****

Ellen blamed Marguerite for nearly everything that was wrong at the Florida Forest, even things that had happened before Marguerite got there, but she was correct in her assumption that Marguerite had been behind the written reprimand she received.

It was written in standard office memo format, printed out on an ink jet printer upon watermarked corporate letterhead. With both eyes and mouth widening, Ellen began to read:

FROM: Corporate Headquarters, Personnel Division

TO: Ellen Patrick, Staff Nurse

DATE: April 3, 1997

cc: Employee File

RE: Inappropriate Employee Relations

It has come to the attention of this office that your recent actions indicate an improper and inappropriate relationship with a fellow employee, namely peer Nurse Iselin.

It is the policy of this company to strongly discourage intimate relationships between employees. As Mr. Iselin is your peer and not a subordinate, your actions do not directly violate our zero-tolerance stance on the issue of sexual harassment. Nonetheless, your conduct has implications that impact your position as a Staff Nurse.

It is not the policy of this company to dictate moral beliefs to our employees, but we have found that inappropriate personal relations between employees is not so much a "moral" issue as it is one of "morale". Such relationships affect the morale of the entire "team".

Continued disruption of company morale may lead to further disciplinary action, up to and including termination of employment.

"This is unbelievable," Ellen said. "It's unreal. How can they even talk about morals and morale after what's happened to this place? This is nonsense. It's ridiculous. It's stupid."

"It's horseshit," agreed Michael.

"You know what, Mike? I'm not even going to worry about it. That's right. When you consider where it's coming from, it's too stupid to even take seriously. It's laughable."

Michael did not find it laughable. When two days went by and he had not received a similar reprimand, he penned his own two-word resignation.

"Fuck off," it read.

Marguertie Cannon did not plead with Michael to stay.

****

THE PRAYER OF ALL NURSES: Dear Lord, make me always a nurse and never a judge. A prostitute with needle tracks is no less entitled to dignified care than a nun with human service awards. Never let me feel superior to those entrusted in my care. Amen.

****

The Florida Forest was finally sold to new owners.

State governments will rarely shut down a nursing home outright. To do so would displace too many frail patients too quickly.

Instead, the troubled facility is subjected to fines, freezes, cuts and moratoriums. Ellen figured that these actions must be intended to penalize the company, for they certainly could not be meant to help the residents.

By the time the new owners entered the building, the Florida forest had been under a moratorium for four months. And for four months there had been no money for the residents.

Ellen would always believe that it would have been more humane to have shut down the Florida Forest outright.

The newest new owner was another private healthcare management company. This one seemed different from the last. Certainly, Robin James seemed different from the last. A High Heels with a heart, Ellen would eventually admit.

When Sister Mary Kate left the Florida Forest, it was one of the few facilities in the area that held the State's Superior rating. By the time Robin James got there a year and a half later, the State was threatening to shut it down.

As is usually the case in these matters, it would take longer for the Florida Forest to improve than it had taken for it to deteriorate.

It would be months before the facility would be restored to Standard. And it would never again be rated as a Superior skilled nursing and rehabilitation center.

****

Robin James had inherited 378 residents. Many of the residents and their families had bailed out months ago and the State had put a freeze on any new admissions. Robin started with 122 empty beds.

She decided to concentrate first on the 378 residents she did have.

Some of the residents were underweight and dehydrated. Some had bedsores. Robin knew that these problems would improve only with adequate staff and adequate supplies.

She could offer attractive enough salary and benefit packages to recruit quality caregivers, but if she did that, she wouldn't be able to offer the existing staff any more than they already had.

Robin had a hunch that the staff that had stayed over the past year had stayed for reasons other than money. And she would have to hope her hunch was correct this afternoon, when she would meet with the employees to tell them the truth about the facility's financial situation.

Robin James was an experienced nursing home administrator with a good track record for maintaining standards of patient care. The problems facing her were not insurmountable. The nutritional status of most residents could be restored with enough caregivers. And even the worst bedsore, Robin knew, could usually be healed within six months. These were temporary problems to which she had solutions.

But there were other things wrong at the Florida Forest, things that Robin James could not so easily place her finger upon.

Over the past year, the nursing staff had watched their beloved residents wither under their care. They doubted Robins's sincerity. Indeed, many had come to doubt themselves.

And the residents, more vulnerable even than children in their frailty, had come to doubt that they would ever again receive good care. Some doubted that anyone cared about them at all.

These were the wounds that would take much longer to heal.

****

THE NURSING PRAYER WE ARE ASHAMED OF: Dear Lord, don't let him die on my shift.

****

Nurses have a secret nomenclature by which they classify patients during shift reports. At first glance, this practice seems arbitrary and insensitive. Actually, it is, but no one ever said that nurses were perfect. Before you begin your med pass, you should know which of your patients are Crushes, Tubes, Cubes, Baby Dolls, Walkie-Talkies, A&OX3, Confused, Crashes, Boo-Boos, Sugars, Bugs, Quads, Seekers or Young.

Crushes are patients who must receive their medication in crushed or liquid form. They generally experience a physical inability to swallow normally, although some are simply too confused to swallow safely.

Crushes require a special level of care. Depending upon their condition they may also require all fluids to be thickened to honey or nectar consistency. These patients can easily aspirate fluid into their lungs and something as innocuous as a glass of water can be deadly to them.

Tubes are patients who receive their food and medication through tubes. There are nasal tubes, gastric tubes and tubes that empty directly into the small intestine.

Cubes are patients who have developed decubitus ulcers, or bedsores. Enough has been said already about decubitus.

To Ellen, the most touching of all patients were the Baby Dolls. Baby Dolls neither walked nor talked, although many smiled and some cried. They had to be fed, bathed and dressed. They were almost always Crushes and often Tubes and the most likely of all patients to become Cubes.

The antithesis of a Baby Doll is a Walkie-Talkie. These patients can walk and talk and quite often (but not always) are also A&OX3. To qualify as A&OX3, a patient must be able to verbalize who they are, where they are and what era they live in.

Some patients can walk, but they cannot talk. It is wise to begin with the assumption that they are also A&OX3.

Patients who are not A&OX3 are Confused. Confusion happens for many reasons and not all confusion is permanent or consistent.

Nurses who worked the Sunshine Unit were sharply aware that even a patient who has been confused for years may suddenly have episodes of A&OX3. The nursing staff who had been on the Sunshine Unit for awhile recognized that this could be a sign of the patient's impending death.

Crashes are patients who have fallen, gotten into a fight, or in some other way been the subject of an Incident Report within the past 72 hours. Crashes must be assessed every shift for symptoms of infection or neurological damage.

Crashes are often also Boo-Boos, or those patients who require dressing changes.

Sugars are diabetic patients. If you work the floor, make sure your aides know the difference between the symptoms of high blood glucose and the symptoms of low blood glucose.

Bugs are patients who are receiving medication for "bugs" or infections. Bugs must be monitored for fever, allergic reactions and superinfection (when antibiotics destroy the patient's "good" bacteria).

Quads are quadriplegic patients, or those with a paralyzing injury below the neck. Most were young men who received spinal cord injuries while engaged in high-risk activity. Many were angry. Some were depressed. These were the patients that Ellen found the most challenging, although most grew to trust her over time.

Seekers were patients who were continuously seeking pain medication. These were patients without a diagnosis to support their complaints of pain and who often watched the clock for the next dosage time. Many did not appear to be in pain at all. These were the patients that Ellen found the most frustrating to deal with. She was torn between not wanting a patient to suffer and not wanting to contribute to an addiction. Her only recourse was to consult with the doctor, but sometimes the doctors didn't seem sure what to do either.

****

A young resident in a nursing home is anyone under the age of 70, but Young residents are in their 20s. If they were any younger, they'd be pediatric patients.

Of all the patients at the Florida Forest, it was the Young ones that Ellen never fully recovered from.

Cecilia Montage was Young. Twenty five years old, she must have been beautiful in the days before HIV destroyed her immune system.

What struck Ellen most was her eyes. Wide, dark and ever so slightly slanted, they grabbed you in a way that you dared not look away.

Cecelia was familiar with the red light district just around the corner from the Florida Forest. She had, in fact, grown up in the neighborhood that just edged the district.

Cecilia's mother, a strong Baptist woman, single-handedly raised four daughters in the Church. She fought to keep her little girls away from the drugs and gangs that kept creeping closer and closer to the old neighborhood.

And it looked as if she had succeeded until Cecelia, at the age of 17, developed the nasal passages of an Electrolux. So severe was her cocaine addiction that she turned to theft and, later, prostitution to support her habit.

Cecelia's mother was so ashamed of her that she disowned her, but some members of the church offered to pay for her stay in a local drug rehabilitation hospital. Cecelia was strong enough and whole enough to beat her cocaine addiction. Six years later, she started getting sick.

****

Cecelia refused her medicine regime, which consisted mostly of hard-to-swallow vitamin supplements.

"I don't want any of that shit," she told Ellen. "What is any of that going to do? Call my social worker lady and ask her what she's done about getting me my AZT. She said she'd try to get it for me."

And the social worker was trying, but AZT was an exorbitantly costly medicine and by this time, Cecelia was indigent. The social worker had

151

over 100 cases of indigent people needing exorbitantly costly medicine.

And so Cecelia had to wait. And while she waited, she refused not only medicine but physical and occupational therapy as well.

Smoking in private rooms was prohibited at the Florida Forest, but the nurses often smelled smoke or saw ground out cigarettes on Cecelia's windowsill.

"Look," Ellen said. "If you want a cigarette, I'll help you get out to the porch and give you a light. But if the fire marshal pops in here and sees you smoking, we get hit with a fine. And you could be asked to leave the facility!"

"I don't know where that butt came from," Cecelia answered, looking straight into Ellen's eyes. "Must have been the housekeeper lady."

A couple of times, the nurses thought they smelled marijuana in Cecelia's room, a sensory experience they decided to ignore. On those occasions, Cecelia rested better and vomited less.

What disturbed Ellen most was not Cecelia's refusal to heed medical advice or to follow rules or even to obey laws. It was her refusal to eat.

"C'mon, Cecelia," Ellen urged. "You tell me you want AZT, so obviously you want to live. How can you live if you don't eat?"

"You eat it," she told Ellen.

"Cecelia ...."

"I really don't want that, Nurse Lady. Thank you very much anyway but my mother is bringing my lunch today."

She said that every day but Cecelia's mother never came.

Ten days after Cecelia's admission to the Florida Forest, the regional hospital contacted the facility to inform them that Cecelia's recent chest X-ray was suspicious for tuberculosis.

Cecelia, like all residents of the Florida Forest, had been tested for tuberculosis upon admission. She had tested negative.

The PPD is the standard TB testing tool and it reveals only if the person has ever been exposed to the bacteria. The result is dependent upon the reaction of the body's T-cells. People with AIDS do not have enough T-cells to produce a positive reaction.

"We should have known," Robin James said. "God knows how many residents and staff may have been exposed to TB by now."

"I should have known," Ellen said later to Heidi, the nurse who was working North Wing that day. Since the new owners had taken over at least two medication nurses were assigned per wing on the day shift. Ellen usually worked with Heidi.

"You should have known, I should have known .... that new infection control nurse they brought in here damn sure should have known!" Heidi answered. "But the truth is, none of us did."

"Why didn't we know?" Ellen asked. "AIDS has been around for something like 15 years now. And there's not one word in our policy and procedures about TB screening for AIDS patients."

Heidi shrugged. "Probably because this is a nursing home and not many of our residents are admitted for AIDS. Lord, girl, don't take it so hard. We can't know everything."

Cecelia was admitted to the hospital for further testing. She did not have tuberculosis but she did have pneumocystis carinii pneumonia. Pneumocystis carinii is a protozoa that infects the lungs of people with weak immune systems. It poses virtually no threat to healthy people and the nurses at the Florida Forest knew that.

Nonetheless, some of the staff were now fearful, many were distrustful of the new administration and a few refused to believe Robin James when she insisted that Cecelia did not have tuberculosis.

Several nurses and respiratory therapists refused to work with Cecelia without a specially designed TB mask and Cecelia refused treatment from anyone who wore one.

"I don't have TB!" she cried. "I have AIDS, but I don't have any damned TB!"

Her condition deteriorated and soon she required respiratory suctioning. She continues to refuse treatment from anyone wearing a TB mask. In the end, Ellen was one of the few who would work with her.

One morning Ellen arrived to find Cecelia in such dire need of suctioning that Ellen was amazed she hadn't suffocated in the night.

"I'm still fighting to live, Nurse Lady," she managed to say after Ellen had sufficiently cleared her respiratory passages. "Call my social l worker lady. She said she'd help me get my AZT."

Ellen promised that she would. As she stepped out into the hall, one of the new nurses, a pretty young woman named Vanessa, confronted her.

"You just went in there without a mask! Did you even bother to wash your hands? I just don't see how, as a nurse, you can go in there and expose yourself and everyone else to God knows what!"

"And I don't see how you, as a nurse, can let her drown in her own sections because you won't take off a mask designed for a disease she doesn't have!" Ellen fired back.

Two days later, in the type of snafu that is not uncommon, the Board of Health notified the Florida Forest of Cecelia's suspicious-for-TB state. It was a duplicate notice, the original had arrived weeks ago.

To complicate matters, Cecelia's latest test results (the ones that showed she was free of the disease) had not yet been entered in the central computer. Cecelia was ordered back to the hospital isolation unit. When she was discharged two days later she refused to go back to the Florida Forest.

Ellen contacted the hospital and spoke with one of Cecelia's nurses. The nurse told her, "She

156

said 'If the Florida Forest doesn't want me then I don't want them."

Ellen called Cecelia's mother, who lived just three blocks from the Florida Forest.

"No, I don't know where she is. I raised four daughters and three of them turned out just fine. Please, just leave me alone."

Ellen took to driving around what she knew to be Cecelia's old neighborhood late at night, hoping to find the emaciated young woman.

"And do what??" Michael exclaimed. "Are you nuts? You'll get your throat slit by crackheads driving around there late at night before you'll ever find her. And if you did find her, what would you do?"

"I don't know. Talk to her, I guess. Michael, she was treated like a leper."

"Ellen, you are going too far. You're crossing the line, you're getting personally involved ...."

"And you haven't?" she cut in. "Don't give me that "personally involved" crap. We all do it! Didn't you make a new TV mysteriously appear in Mr. Burns' room after someone stole his?"

"So I bought him a television set. So what? I wasn't putting my life in jeopardy! Ellen, listen. Maybe you need to take a break from that place. I know I did."

Ellen did not reply.

A week later Ellen read Cecelia's obituary in the newspaper. She had not known until then that Cecelia had had a son.

Twenty five staff members who had been identified as having had any sort of contact with Cecelia were testing for exposure to tuberculosis. All tested negative.

Notice of preliminary approval to finance Cecelia's AZT therapy arrived in the mail a week after her death.

****

Michael disliked calling Ellen at home because her daughter Melissa would usually be the one to answer the phone. It wasn't that Melissa was rude. Quite the opposite. She was pointedly, exquisitely and excruciatingly polite. It had been eight months now and the girl had not warmed up to him.

But on that night in May, Michael hear fear in Melissa's voice as she exclaimed, "Oh, Michael, I don't know where she is! She said not to worry, that she'd be back, but she's been acting so weird lately."

"Weird how?"

"Well, not weird but .... I don't know. Like depressed and mad at the same time."

Michael was silent for a moment, then answered slowly "I think I know where she might be."

"Then let's go. Take me there now! I want to find her, Michael .... something's wrong. Come over and get me!"

"Uh-uh. You're not going."

"Why not? She's my mother!"

"Uh-uh. Stay right where you are and with a little luck I'll be there shortly with your mother."

"Michael!" Melissa hollered, but he was gone.

****

Ellen's car wasn't hard to spot, Michael thought as he pulled into the space beside it. It was the only late model vehicle on the block.

She wasn't hard to spot, either, standing at the intersection of two streets. Neither of which, he thought, she has any business being on.

She didn't notice him approaching her. Michael wondered if he would ever stop being amazed at how beautiful she looked, if her face would ever become ordinary to him.

But her beauty was like a mask under the streetlight tonight. Her features were frozen in what he recognized as grief.

He cleared his throat. "Stand here much longer and a couple of hookers are going to kick your ass for standing in their territory."

She didn't answer him. She scarcely seemed to notice him. Across the street a woman that Michael was pretty sure was a hooker whistled.

"Ellen, look at me," he said.

She did and he saw that her face was whiter than her uniform.

"I'm trying to see what it felt like," she said.

Her voice was strained and unnatural. She was speaking too rapidly. He searched her eyes for signs of drug use and found none.

What he did find caused him to taste metal in his mouth. A brief memory of being robbed at gunpoint years back flashed in his mind. It had been so long since he'd felt fear this intensely that at first he did not recognize it.

Ellen's eyes were no longer blue. They were the cold gray of iron and they looked utterly lifeless.

"I want to know what it felt like," she continued. "To stand out here night after night, trying to make a damned living." She laughed then. It was a harsh, ugly sound. "And so far, I haven't gotten one decent offer."

"Maybe it's the uniform," Michael said softly and Ellen's laughter went high-pitched and hysterical.

And then the dam broke. Raw, ragged emotion flowed out of her with such intensity that Michael feared they would both be swept away by it. He lost all sense of time then and had no idea how long they stood there with the hookers watching them curiously from across the street.

Ellen was weeping copiously but she was not incoherent. He understood every word she said.

"We're all whores, Michael, in one way or another. Anyone who could work at that place for money was prostituting their own soul. And she was treated like she was less than human. Here we are, we're supposed to know everything and be everything to everyone and we can't even give the most basic, simple ...."

"She's gone, honey. Let it go."

And she let him hold her then and he spoke softly to her. Later, neither of them could remember what he had said but his words had an almost magical effect on her. Later, Michael would remember that it felt almost as if some supernatural force was helping him, putting eloquent words in his mouth at the time when he didn't have any idea of what to say.

And then it was over and Ellen was pulling away from him.

"Why are you always so composed?" she asked, with a hint of resentment. Her eyes were blue and alive again.

Michael understood. She had let him see her at her weakest, most vulnerable, most unstable worst. And if he didn't do something to make her feel righteous again she would never forgive him for it.

"Natural male superiority," he answered easily.

"Yeah, right."

"Absolutely. Mental and physical superiority, which I will use to haul your ass out of here if you ever again do something this stupid, Ellen."

"Oh no. Don't start that with me. We were doing just fine, Michael. You don't have to come across like some Neanderthal, prehistoric, macho .... uh ...."

"Pig," he supplied. "I'm a macho male pig. I believe that's the word you were looking for."

"No, it wasn't" she snapped. "But it will do just fine. Excuse me." Ellen brushed past him.

"Where are you going?"

"To my car. And you don't have to walk me there, either. I'm a lot tougher than you think."

Michael knew how tough she could be. She was stomping away from him now, her stride furious. She stormily squared her shoulders. Even her ponytail looked angry. He waited until she had walked about 20 feet away from him.

"You have a great butt, Ellen," he said.

Ellen whirled around and Michael ran.

And from far, far away Robert Bishop watched them wrestle. He often watched over the two nurses who had been so conscientious with the morphine, who had made sure he hadn't suffered too horribly during his last days on Earth.

"You idiot," Ellen managed to say before Michael covered her mouth with his, his kiss flooding her with warmth and making her new again.

And Michael knew, right then and there, that she would be the last woman he would ever love.

They walked to their cars then, her hand in his. They were still arguing.

Robert Bishop smiled beatifically. Through a most privileged communication, he knew that they would be together, arguing like that, for the next 40 years.

****

"They're back," Jason said. "I recognize your mom's car."

Melissa went to the window and stared out at Michael and her mother. Her mother's face looked puffy, like she'd been crying for a long time, but she looked serene. Gratitude and jealousy mixed uneasily in Melissa as she watched Michael put his arm around her mother.

Ellen's blue eyes snapped brightly at Melissa the moment she saw Jason. "And who said you could have your boyfriend over here when I'm not home?"

Melissa was silent for a moment and then said, "Uh, Michael, this is Jason, my boyfriend. Jason, this is Michael, my mom's boyfriend."

Jason and Michael shook hands while Ellen waited for Melissa to answer her question.

"I'm waiting, Melissa."

"I was scared, Mom. I didn't want to be alone! You think we did anything with me being this upset? Where were you, anyway? ....I'm waiting, Mom."

"Jason, my man," Michael said, "I think here's where we're supposed to go off and chase women and talk football or something. I'm sure you're too young to drink. How do you feel about near beer?"

And after they were gone, Melissa whirled around, her own blue eyes snapping brightly at her mother.

"Where were you, Mom?"

"Not yet. First things first. You are not, I repeat, not to have Jason in here when I'm not home. Not even again, Melissa."

"Fine. And you are not to ever again take off like you did tonight."

"Deal," Ellen agreed.

They fell silent then and Melissa busied herself with making hot chocolate, the kind with the mini marshmallows already in the mix. They never gave you enough in the package, Melissa thought, as she opened the cupboard to get out the bag of mini marshmallows her mother always bought.

"Want one?" she asked and Ellen nodded. Melissa handed her a cup of hot chocolate and they both sat down at the kitchen table.

"Mom?"

"Yes?"

"Is the reason you don't want Jason in here when your're not home is that your're afraid I'll end up pregnant?"

"It's one of the reasons, yes."

"Like you did?"

"Yes," Ellen admitted. :"Like I did."

"Do you regret it?"

Ellen stared at the melting marshmallow mountain in her cup. "Do I regret having a baby when I was still a kid myself? Yes, I do. I could have given you so much more if I'd been more financially stable and more mature. But do I regret having you, Melissa? Never in a million years. It was the most beautiful thing I ever did by accident."

Melissa smiled. "Ah, you didn't do so bad for a young mom."

"And you didn't do so bad for a young baby."

"Mom?"

"Yes?"

"Where were you tonight?"

And Ellen explained it to her as best as she could, for the memory was already starting to feel like something far away, almost like a dream.

And Melissa mostly understood, for she was 16 now and fast becoming more woman than child.

And as she listened to Ellen talk, Melissa realized with a soft, hollow shock that Michael had clearly known a side of her mother that Melissa had not known existed.

If he hadn't, he wouldn't have known where to find her.

If no one had found her, if she'd stayed out on the street much longer .... Melissa shuddered, not allowing herself to complete the thought.

"And now of course Michael thinks I need a vacation," Ellen was saying. "Isn't that just like a man?"

"I agree with him, Melissa said.

"Oh great," Ellen groaned. "Now both of you are going to gang up on me."

Melissa grinned in a way that made her look exactly like Ellen.

And it was with Robin James' blessing that Ellen took a long vacation before she returned to work at the Florida Forest. It probably wasn't long enough but it was better than nothing at all.

And Melissa was never again pointedly polite to Michael.

****

"Miss Vaughn, we have to hurry," Tasha urged. "The press will be here soon."

"The press! Whatever for?"

"Your birthday. They're going to do a little piece on your birthday."

"My birthday! Good heavens, why?"

"Because, Miss Vaughn, not many people live to be 105 years old."

"Nor should they," Stella answered.

Tasha combed Stella's hair straight back and styled it into a topknot. Don't forget your teeth, Miss Vaughn," she said.

Nag, nag, nag, Stella thought. Her memory was probably better than Tasha's.

The press was waiting for them when Tasha wheeled Stella into the main dayroom. To Stella's amazement, there were reporters from five different television stations and three newspapers.

This was going to be worse than when she and John got married.

"I still say it must be an awfully slow news day," she whispered to Tasha".

The cake was waiting and the staff sang Happy Birthday to her. On cue, Stella managed to blow out the single candle and was applauded as if she had hit a home run.

"Mrs. Vaughn, how does it feel to be the oldest woman in the city?"

"Amazing."

"Look this way, Stella. Smile!"

"Mrs. Vaughn, what is your secret to a long life?"

"Well, if I told it wouldn't be a secret, now would it?"

This reporter was young, female and sweet-looking. Earnestly, she said "Mrs. Vaughn, maybe you could share some information about your lifestyle with our readers."

"Well," Stella replied thoughtfully. "Everything in moderation, as my grandma used to say." "The other reporters gathered around.

"You see," she continued. "I've always eaten whatever I wanted but never too much. I've never gone on a diet. Whatever for? Don't eat so much and you won't need to go on a diet. I've always been active but I've never killed myself exercising. In my day, the only time anyone ever saw me run was if something was chasing me. I drink a little .... keeps the blood thin, you know ....but I never get drunk. What's the sense in getting drunk when life is so intoxicating just as it is?"

The reporters were taking in her every word.

"And so," the sweet-looking reporter said. "Your secret to a long life is to take everything in moderation?"

"Well, there is one more thing."

"Miss Vaughn ...." Tasha warned, but Stella ignored her.

"What?" asked the young woman.

Stella motioned for the reporter to move closer.

"Miss Vaughn!" Tasha hissed, but Stella whispered in the reporter's ear. The reporter turned a deep shade of crimson.

"Course, I don't imagine you'd be printing that in a family newspaper," Stella said as the reporter gathered up her materials. "But I wanted you to have the whole story, seeing how you're a newswoman and all."

"Miss Vaughn!" Tasha whispered fiercely.

"Oh, don't be such a fuddy-duddy," Stella told her.

Stella looked around. Most of her friends at the Florida Forest were here, as well as a few of her enemies. She smiled warmly at Frances Goshen. After all, the poor woman had liked Robert Bishop, too. Maybe even loved him. And there was absolutely no sense in being jealous over a dead man.

Most of her favorite staff members were there, too, even the ones who no longer worked at the Florida Forest. Why, there was that sweet Mary and that nice Ellen and even that young man nurse Ellen went with.

"When are you two going to get married?" she greeted them.

"Soon," Michael promised. "And we'll invite you to the wedding."

"Well, you'd better hurry. How much time do you think I've got left?"

"Happy Birthday, Miss Vaughn," Tasha said, hugging her. "I love you"

"I love you too, darlilng," Stella answered, hugging her back.

Looking across the room, Stella caught they eye of Bill Frankton. Bill lived on the East Wing and he and Stella occasionally played Yatzhee together.

My, Stella thought. How handsome he looks in that new vest today.

Funny, she'd never noticed before how nice his eyes were.

And even thought they'd already had the cake, Stella closed her eyes and made a wish.

THE END.

****

EPILOGUE

Through laughter and sorrow

Through sunshine and rain

Earth's bitter loss

Is Heaven's sweet gain.

Posted on the online memorial for Michael Thomas
Iselin, March 28, 2020

****

It was New Year's Day and yellow and pink showers of tubuia flowers were falling from the trees. Ellen remembered when they didn't even bloom until early spring but the tabuias, along with the magnolias and the bottlebrush, were flowering earlier and earlier every year until even the most adamant admitted that maybe the seasons were growing warmer.

Still it was winter and Ellen had a cough. Since the pandemic that had ripped through her world, she no longer shrugged off mild symptoms. The chest Xray revealed only degenerative changes in her thoracic spine. She knew that meant her vertebrae were shrinking. That she was shrinking. After decades of caring for old women Ellen was

174

mildly surprised to learn that she was becoming one herself.

She didn't really mind. The stunning feminine beauty she had owned in her youth had certainly granted her power but it had also obstructed others from seeing her clearly. By now, she had completed what her mother's generation had called The Change. It had begun with feeling as if her hair was on fire and ended with her torso shaped less like a violin and more like a refrigerator. Her beautiful ivory skin did not hold its elasticity well but she accepted the naturalness of aging. Ellen was neither ashamed nor dismayed by her changing body but she wished she felt more of the wisdom that she was certain she should have by now.

****

The virus had entered Ellen's unit one spring afternoon when the pink and white azaleas were blooming outside the window and the air had turned warm. By 2020 Ellen had been a nurse for long enough to have born witness to hundreds of deaths. But not like this. Dear God, not like this! This virus killed within hours and Michael, her beloved Michael, was the Florida Forest's first fatality. This despite the fact that Michael was neither elderly nor a patient. Michael came home from work one night with a scratchy throat and died almost before COVID-19 was a household word.

Ellen didn't cry, not for years. She screamed. Her wellspring of sorrow was so deep that it spilled over into wild sounds. Fearing she would alarm her neighbors she took to driving on the highway when she felt the screams coming. With music blasting and windows down she purged all of the grief from her open throat until the next time.

After three years she stopped screaming. A year after that she traded her Camry in for a smaller Corolla. She was alone now and didn't need so much space but she felt a twinge of guilt knowing that someone else would drive the Camry. She was sure that all of that pain was somehow stuck in the upholstery.

****

HEAVENLY INTERLUDE

Text message between Michael Iselin and a most privileged communication date March 28, 2020:

Hey I just got here

Hey

WTF? I was supposed to be with her for 40 years.

Yeah sorry

What happened??????

The pandemic. We didn't see it coming

Fair enough Neither did we

****

The loss of Michael was the most traumatizing aspect of the pandemic for Ellen but it wasn't the most surreal.

Watching patients get sick and even die of something they swore was fake was bizarre but even that wasn't the strangest part. No, what made Ellen feel as if she had stepped into the Twilight Zone happened shortly after Michael had died. By then, people had become afraid to hug or even stand close together but Melissa grabbed Ellen and hugged her tightly. And Ellen hugged back all the while thinking "Dear Lord, of all the stupid things I have done in my life please don't let hugging my daughter be the thing that kills me.

Time passed as time always does. After a time, the pandemic became endemic. Somewhat like the flu although Covid didn't seem to have a particular season. People got vaccinated or not, got sick or not. Ellen lost a few patients and a few friendships. Most people did. Viruses are tiny but oh they are mighty.

****

Ellen retired just after the peak of the pandemic. She was only 60 but the years of illness and pain and death and sorrow had exhausted her. She didn't regret having been a nurse but she didn't regret not being one any longer either.

****

And so Ellen spent her time gardening and playing with the grandchildren. She never forgot Michael but in time she learned to shift the weight of her grief so that she could walk through the rest of her life. Besides, she hadn't spent all those years caring for the dying without learning a thing or two. There is more than science can explain and Ellen knew it was more than possible that she would see Michael again someday.

Made in the USA
Las Vegas, NV
01 December 2024

12734723R00105